I0600941

An Unsated Thirst

S.W. Campbell

Published by Shawn Campbell

Cover photograph taken by Mallory Anderson

An Unsated Thirst

ISBN: 978-0-9977105-7-1

To my friends, the ones who say what I need to hear rather than what I want to hear.

An Unsated Thirst

Table Of Contents

Preface

Within the pages of *An Unsated Thirst* are forty-one of my earliest written short stories and other writings, with the majority penned between August of 2010 and March of 2013.

I first started writing when I was a kid, the late childhood and awkward adolescent years, writing mostly fantasy stories filled with orcs and wizards and Star Wars fan fiction, which was exactly as good as you would imagine it to be. It wasn't really anything anybody would want to read, but I enjoyed it, so I filled a couple dozen spiral notebooks with a barely legible scrawl. I grew up in the middle of nowhere, about a twenty-three mile drive from the nearest grocery store and a two hour drive from the nearest town of any significant size, so I had a lot of time by myself to think up stories.

I kept it up until I started high school, and then promptly abandoned it to unsuccessfully pursue hormonal urges and rather sad attempts at being cool. What little writing I did do were rather sad attempts at poetry which I'm glad to say I burned upon turning twenty. In college I had a short resurgence and the first hints that maybe writing was something I was actually good at. After turning in a story called *Golden Tears* for my English 102 class, I was rather surprised when a friend in another class told me that my instructor had read it in front of them as an example of what a good short story should be. The instructor never said a single thing about it to me, but it left me with the sense that this was something I could actually do, though not the want to actually do it.

Aside from a few essays, which though creative have no business being published, the only thing I wrote during this period of any merit was the basis of what became the story *On Top Of The World*. I also wrote half of the epic history of the fantasy world I had created in my childhood in a fashion similar to J.R.R. Tolkien's *Silmarillion*, but luckily for us all, it met its final fate with a single click on the word delete. Such thoughts of writing died with it, and so ended what I thought of at the time as nothing more than a childhood fancy.

I didn't really start writing again until the end of the summer of 2010, mostly because I was going through a bunch of crap revolving around a relationship gone bad, which looking back, now seems like a really bad cliché. The writing at first was exactly what you'd expect to come from such a start, but over time it evolved into something other people would actually want to read. Many of these early stories were nothing more than venting, which later led to several failed attempts to write a book, the remains of which make up most of the very short stories contained within this collection.

The first short story to be written independent from these beginnings was *The Colonel* in August of 2012, which was based on a conversation I had with a friend. What followed was a veritable explosion of writing of both the independent and angst-ridden variety. To be frank, it felt great to get things out of my mind and onto paper, by which I mean on a computer screen. Since the writing of *The Colonel* I have written at least one short story a month up to the present day, and to date have written 182 stories.

I first started sending my short stories to literary reviews in early 2013, after my friend Adrianna, who somehow convinced me to let her read my stuff, talked me into it. It started with just a few writing contests, but when I got back some really nice reviews, I decided that maybe I had some stuff worth getting out there so I jumped in whole hog. I got my first acceptance for the story *Doing What You Have To Do* after thirty-eight rejections. However, the accepting literary review soon after went out of business before it could be published. It took another 140 rejections before I got another story approved, *The Heartbreaker* (which is not in this collection), and actually published. Though today I have close to 1,500 rejections under my belt, I also have fourteen stories published, including four presented in this collection. In addition, I have self-published a full-length novel entitled *The Uncanny Valley*, and two bathroom books called *Professor Errare Presents 45 Jerks And Counting* and *Professor Errare Presents 40 American Jackasses Worth Knowing*. While my writing certainly has not led to any riches, it has certainly been one hell of a ride.

They say that an author's first stories are their most raw, which is something that I most certainly agree with. Re-reading through many of these old stories I found myself cringing, not just at the quality of the writing, but also at the subjects chosen. It took me quite some time to decide to include many of the stories presented here in *An Unsated Thirst*. Angst is the word that comes to mind with several. However, in the end I decided that they were all worth including. I know that how many of them are viewed will be dependent upon the mood of the reader, with the emotion ranging from a feeling of connection to an over exaggerated eye roll. But in the end, I hope that it's remembered that even the most cringeworthy of the stories in this collection are ones with which we can all identify. Though we try to forget such parts of our lives, they are an important part of the whole. Hence their inclusion in this of what will be the first of many short story collections.

I hope you enjoy *An Unsated Thirst* as much as I have enjoyed writing and putting it together. Some of the stories are biographical, some are fictional, and some are a combination of the two. I'll leave it to the reader to decide which is which. However, for the sake of my parents, who have shown me nothing but love and support, I'll state right now that the story *Major Wilkins Comes Home* has absolutely no basis in my own life. Happy reading.

Angst

I have been told by some people that you do not understand why I am so upset and hurt over this whole thing. I am upset because I fell in love and cared deeply for you, and you hurt me more than anybody has ever hurt me before. I am upset because I gave up things I enjoyed to be with you, things that I cannot get back. I am upset because you claim you want to be friends, but friends provide comfort while you only give me pain. I am upset because you treat me like someone you only went on a couple of casual dates with, not someone who shared a lot of personal things with you and listened to many of your own very personal things. I am upset because I should have walked away when the problems first began, but I loved you.

Most of all I am upset because I do not understand, and you do nothing to help me understand. You will not talk with me, and only get mad if I bring it up. The start was like a dream, and at least to me, everything seemed to be going great. At the time I would have done anything for you, and accepted you no matter what you may have told me, but then I left on my trip and without warning, silence.

Upon my return I found out about what had happened at the campout. You tried to break up, but let me talk you out of it. But you never would tell me why, beyond saying you had anxiety. It was like an excuse, never saying what you felt anxiety about. What thoughts were pushing you into such a state. I did everything I could think of to try and help you, but it is impossible to deal with a problem when you don't even know what the problem is. I've never talked to someone for so long, about so many things, without ever once talking about what needed to be talked about.

I was, and still am hurt and confused. I could do nothing but watch as your silence filled me with anxiety and depression, eroding my self-confidence and light-heartedness until there was nothing left. Watching as day by day you became less attracted to me, your silence destroying the things that you were originally attracted to, an attraction that once amazed me with its intensity. Each day seeing the sadness in your eyes, and feeling the same in my own, knowing I could do nothing, waiting for you to talk. Finally letting you push me away. Hearing your excuses of anxiety and no longer being attracted to me, never learning how things had gone so wrong. I would have accepted anything if it was explained to me, but was never given the chance. Instead I was given silence, and contempt for needing more, for having emotions.

I am upset because you promised to try and instead used that time to make leaving me behind easier for you, only adding to my pain. I am upset because I once believed you cared about me, but yet seem not to care how cruel your actions were. I am hurt, and neither time nor people offer me any comfort. I do not know what happened. To me it is like a switch was flipped.

You offer me no comfort, no closure, you do not help me understand. You have made all my fears, fears that kept me from relationships in the past, come true. I am upset, because you want me to move on, act like nothing ever happened between us, but give me no way to move on except hating you. I am upset because I still care for you. I did nothing wrong, but have been severely punished. I am in hell.

Doing What You Have To Do

The boy sits on the tailgate of the pickup, dangling his feet and kicking them back and forth, pretending the furtive motion pushes the machinery and metal forward on its slow journey up the road. He sucks in a deep breath, feigning to take a drag from an imaginary cigarette, and blows out, his breath steaming forth through the frigid air. A soft bump on the rough road jolts him slightly. He clutches tighter to the precious cargo sitting on the tailgate next to him. The feeling of it makes his skin crawl. His hands feel dirty and he desperately wants to wash them.

An old black angus cow walks behind, steam intermittently blasting from her nostrils. The cow walks with her head low, her ears drooped, and her shoulders slumped. When they found her in the pasture that morning she had been standing in the same spot for some time, refusing to move from her place of grief. Even now she feels drawn back toward it. She stops moving, and turns to look back up the road from which they had come. The boy lets out a soft low, a plaintive cry that is carried by the wind. The cow turns back and her body regains some of its old shape and stature. She lets out a deeper copy of the boy's call, a pitiful moo tinged with hope. The boy lows again and the cow raises her head and trots to catch up, her oversized bag flopping between her legs, her great belly bouncing with each lumbering step. The boy feels bad for tricking her.

The pickup drives through a gate into a small pen. The boy jumps from the tailgate to the ground slowly passing beneath his feet, and quickly steps aside to let the cow pass before moving back to close the gate. He lifts the loose collection of three wooden posts held together by four strands of barb wire and stretches them across the pen's entrance. His small skinny arms strain beneath his coat as he struggles to loop a wire over the end post to secure the gate. The wires groan and stretch, but not quite far enough. The boy's father gets out of the pickup and calmly walks back to his son at the gate. He reaches over the top of the boy and helps push the post close enough to drop the loop of wire to over it. He turns around and signals for the boy to follow.

The boy walks behind his father, his face red with shame and embarrassment, glad that his father is not looking back at him. He is eleven now, he should be able to close the gate without help. His father steps beside the tailgate of the pickup, his face expressionless, and reaches for the precious cargo, grabbing it by one of its legs. The boy rushes forward to help, grabbing the other leg. He has to prove that the gate was just a fluke. His father gives him a look. The boy knows his father does not want him to be there. The boy ignores the look and together they pull the mass from the tailgate. The dead calf falls to the hard cold earth. Father and son drag it toward the nearby barn, its grieving mother following, mooing softly.

Calving season is one of the most beautiful and magical times on the ranch. The baby calves are dropped unceremoniously into a strange new cold world which they explore with delight and wonder. Despite all the new hardships of life outside the womb they frolic and play, delighting in just being alive. The boy smiles at the thought of the calves playing, a yearly reminder of how special and miraculous life is.

But life can be cruel, and things can go wrong with neither rhyme or reason. The calf they drag through the snow had once been just like all the others, full of life. Now it lies dead, its body stiff and cold, its once shiny black coat matted, its tongue hanging from its jaw, its eyes staring without sight at the world around it. Maybe the calf had become sick and they had failed to notice until it was too late. Perhaps the calf had been born with something wrong with it, a genetic defect for which nothing could be done. The boy hoped that it was the latter. It was best not to contemplate the guilt of knowing that you had failed something that depended on you. These things happen, there is little that can be done, but the boy knew his father would still blame himself for not doing enough.

The pair deposit the dead calf on the dirt floor of the barn's shadowy interior, the only light from the big doorway, and move away from the corpse. The cow moves past them and stands over her lost offspring, sniffing at the thing that once was. She lows softly and her grief crosses the divide of animal and man.

"Wait here, I'll get the stuff and be right back."

The boy's father walks out of the barn and back to the pickup. The boy waits, looking out at the steely clouds marching above the gray hills covered by the dark shapes of junipers and dirty white skiffs of snow hiding in shadows that the sun does not touch. His eyes shift back to the dead calf and saddened mother. The cow looks up at him and her eyes seem to communicate a desperate plea to make things better, a hope that in her ignorance she is mistaken, that things can be set right. The boy looks away back out the barn door, watching the dust motes dance in the muted sunlight.

His father comes back with several lengths of baling twine. Together they grab the calf by its hind legs and drag it into a small side enclosure, shutting the gate behind them so the cow cannot follow. She paces back and forth, unsure. Both man and boy take off their warm cotton gloves and heavy overcoats, stripping down to the hay covered sweatshirts they wear underneath.

The boy's father pulls out a large pocket knife and opens it. The blade does not gleam in the dim light from the barn doorway, it's too old and worn, covered in rust and grime. He takes a rod of steel from his belt and rubs it along the knife's edge, honing the blade, bringing back some of the old sharpness. The boy pulls out his own knife, feeling the weight in his hand. He opens the blade slowly, careful not to cut himself on the razor sharp edge. It is bright and shiny, flashing in the soft light. He holds the knife like the treasured item that it is, a Christmas present from only a few months ago.

The boy's father leans over the dead calf and with a quick thrust creates a hole in one hind leg between the tibia and fibula. The boy watches as his father puts the bloody knife on the ground and loops the twine several times through the hole. A knot secures everything together. The boy's father stands and, reaching above his head, throws the twine over a low rafter. The boy grabs onto the other end as it falls back to earth. Together they pull the calf upward until it hangs completely off the ground at eye level. The boy's father holds the calf in place and the boy secures it with a few twists and knots around a nearby post, his hands moving slowly, nervous under the watchful eyes of the older man.

The man picks up his knife and moves back to the calf, he looks at his son, and the boy can again feel that his father does not want him to be there, does not want him to witness what comes next. With deft sure strokes of the blade he cuts the skin just below the knee of each hind leg. He yanks downward on the loose skin, pulling it away from the muscle beneath, his knife cutting the sinew and tissue. The boy moves forward to help. His father stops his work.

"Be careful to not cut through the hide."

The boy nods. Together they slowly peel the skin from the dead calf's legs, a morbid fruit hanging in the barn. Things feel dark and grotesque, a macabre scene. The body of a young victim slowly mutilated as its worried mother stands on the other side of a gate. The boy has helped skin and dress deer and elk before, but this somehow feels different. There is none of the joy of the hunt in this moment, no elation in this desecration of the dead. The boy tries to tell a joke he heard in school. His voice sounds small, the words far away. His father only grunts and points with his knife.

"Make sure you cut so the tail is attached to the skin. It only works if you have the tail."

The boy nods and the two continue working. In his left hand the boy grips the hide, one side cold and covered in black hair, the other side warm and slick. He pulls the hide downward, away from the body. The boy's right hand holds his knife, which separates the hide from the muscle and fat with slow slicing strokes, applying enough pressure to cut sinew, but not enough to cut through skin. Naked, the calf is a yellowish white, streaked with the red of veins and exposed muscle. It stands out starkly in the shadows of the barn. Blood does not flow from the body. It has been too long.

The boy does not want to be here, he does not want to be part of this terrible spectacle. He keeps his mind blank, his hands working automatically. He does not want to think about what the thing he is skinning once was. He does not want to hear the soft and worried lowing of the cow just outside the gate. His eyes concentrate on his work, each cut steady and careful. He does not want to screw up the job, does not want his father to think that he can't handle helping. His mind retreats and his brain stops thinking. This has to be done, even if he doesn't want to do it.

The boy looks up at the man next to him. His father's rough and scarred hands move with a deftness that the boy cannot hope to match. The skin is slowly pulled downward as if by a machine, the sinew attaching it to the dead calf sliced as though it is butter. The father's mouth sits in a hard line, and his eyes watch both the boy's work and his own at the same time. His eyes see everything, but it is as though they are looking from a long way off. The boy does not want his father to have to face the unpleasant task alone.

The skin hangs down from the calf, like a woman's skirt if she was hung upside down by her legs, revealing what lay hidden beneath. When the knives reach the front legs they are skinned up to just below the knees before the boy's father cuts the hide loose from them. The same operation is done as they reach the neck. With a final jerk of the blade the hide comes completely loose. The boy's father holds the skin, not letting it touch the ground, and reverses it so the soft black hair is once again on the proper side. He hangs the hide from the fence, and cuts a hole along the belly. He lifts it once again and hangs it across his shoulder.

The man nods at his son who cuts the twine where it is attached to the post. The skinned carcass falls to the ground, straw and dust sticking to the exposed muscle. Man and boy clean their knives with straw, close them, and put them back in their pockets. The boy's father gestures with his free hand.

"Go ahead and drag it back out to her."

The boy opens the gate and drags the skinless mass back into the main pen before returning to his father. The cow watches in silence. She walks forward tentatively, sniffing deeply at the skinned corpse. She sniffs again and backs away. This is not her calf, this is not the little miracle she once carried in her womb. The cow does not recognize it anymore, she does not know the smell.

The boy closes the gate behind him and follows his father into another smaller enclosure. Inside a calf lies in a bed of straw beneath a heat lamp. The calf is a bummer, the unfortunate runt in a pair of twins. The calf's mother could not produce enough milk to support both him and his sister, so he was taken away. An orphan of unfortunate circumstance, surviving on powdered milk from a bottle. A kind hand and pseudo-milk, no matter how well given, is never a substitute for a mother's nourishment and a mother's love. He is unlucky, but maybe today his luck will change.

The man and boy grab the calf with gentle but firm hands. The calf struggles at first, frightened by the change in his daily routine, not understanding what is happening. He is not yet big enough to overpower the man and boy. The boy's father forces the cold wet hide over the calf's head, and bends his legs through each of the holes. With the deed done the bummer calf stands shivering in fright, a grisly spectacle dressed in a sweater made from the hide of his fallen brethren. The boy holds the bummer between his knees and softly whispers promises to it that everything will be all right.

The boy's father opens the gate and walks back into the main part of the barn. He grabs the skinless carcass and pulls it back into the small enclosure as the cow watches, her black eyes following his every movement. As soon as he is out of the cow's sight he signals to the boy with a nod. The boy pushes the bummer forward into the main pen and closes the gate. The man and the boy crouch next to each other and peer through the fence.

The bummer is unsure of what to do. He stands next to the closed gate, shivering in his stolen hide. Miserable, he lets out a plaintive moo. The cow's ears jerk in response, a soft low escapes her mouth. The bummer moos again and walks slowly toward the cow. She lows back as he moves closer and lowers her head, sniffing him where the tail and back come together. The cow seems confused, not sure what to think. The smell is familiar, close to something that she had thought she had lost, but also somewhat different. The calf and cow both stand still, not sure what to do.

Minutes tick by, the man and the boy keep quiet. The calf tentatively walks toward the swollen udders of the cow, her sources of nourishment, aching with unclaimed milk. Both the man and boy hold their breath. The calf's soft black nose nuzzles a teat and his tongue slowly licks the end as he draws it into his mouth. The cow gives a slight jerk, then turns her head to sniff at the calf again. The calf begins to draw down deep drinks of milk, some running out of his mouth as frothy white drool. The cow sniffs the calf again. One hind foot rises slightly. The man and boy will it to fall. The cow hesitates and lets her foot drop.

The boy and his father grab their coats and sneak out of the barn, dragging the carcass behind them. With a grunt the two grab the legs, the man on the hind and the boy on the front, and throw it back into the bed of the pickup. It will be taken up a nearby canyon to provide a feast for coyotes and crows. In two days the hide will join the carcass, its use no longer needed. The boy's father climbs into the cab and starts the pickup while the boy walks across the pen and with a strained grunt opens the gate, always easier than closing it. The pickup passes by and he pulls the wires and posts back to the loop of wire that will hold them tight and closed. His face contorts and turns red and sweat beads on his brow as he tries to force the post over far enough to allow the loop of wire to drop over it.

The boy hears the pickup door open behind him. He strains as hard as he can. Not this time, not twice in one day, he can do it. His arms are tired from his efforts with the calf. They strain as hard as they can, a final desperate push towards victory. So close, just half an inch more, so close. The post falls back from the loop of wire, a retreat as his weak eleven year old arms fail in their exertion. Footsteps, leather boots on frozen earth. His father reaches over him and closes the gate with what seems like an invincible ease. The boy does not look at his father. The man puts his hand on the boy's shoulder for a moment, and then walks back to the pickup and climbs in. The rumbling of the engine is strangely loud in the still cold air. The boy looks back at the barn, the sun starting to sink toward the horizon behind it. Inside he can imagine the calf and the cow, both amazed by the strange miracles of the world. The boy smiles, turns, and walks to the pickup.

The Golden Meadow

We all build for ourselves a reality in which we encase our souls, then shutting ourselves away we tell ourselves that this is for the best and that this is the way it has to be to remain happy. Our souls get covered with scars of the past, burnt by old tears and heartache, and we fear the pain. Sometimes from atop the walls we see golden meadows, but we never venture to them, fearing to leave our protective fortress behind.

Why do we hide within our heads, never voicing what is said within? We tell lies to others to protect them from being hurt. We tell lies to ourselves so that we don't have to risk injury outside our walls. These lies add to our walls, making them thicker and higher, becoming our reality. We want to venture out to the golden meadows, but we fear that once we get there they will be desolate and we will be alone.

So we remain within our citadels, telling ourselves that it's better this way. Complementing the sunny weather while gray clouds pour down rain. We convince ourselves that the dreams of the meadow will always remain better than the possibility of a disappointing reality. That the known is better than the unknown. Never willing to open our gates and take that first step unless someone guarantees it will be painless.

I am tired of sitting on my walls, there is no joy within, only the ache of not knowing. I want to venture out and see the golden meadow. And if it is desolate and I do find myself alone, at least I won't have to wonder anymore. Perhaps I'll find the meadow more verdant than I imagined, or twice as dark as my worst fears. But either way I'll have made the journey that can only begin with honest words.

On Top Of The World

"So who's going to the dance with me this Friday? Is it going to be you or Bridgett?"

Leland smiled with a cocky grin he knew Gretchen found charming. She had told him so just the other day, commenting on his dimples as she ran her fingers along them. Gretchen looked at her hands and smiled back in that shy demure way that Leland found irresistible. He knew the answer already. He could see it past the feigned having to think about it. The false pause of modesty, good manners, and one-upmanship. It was all just part of the show. Gretchen looked up and her eyes went from wide innocence to sly vixen in an instant.

"You took Bridgett out last week. It's my turn this week."

Leland let out a little laugh.

"Well, fair is fair."

The team on the other set of bleachers started hooting and clapping. Leland refocused his attention on the game as big Tim Figgins rushed headlong into the first baseman who had caught the ball right before Tim reached the base. Both sides tensed as the dust settled until Tim reached down and pulled the first baseman up. Leland politely clapped with everyone else and then turned his attention back to Gretchen.

Gretchen was a beauty, there was no other way to put it. She had thin delicate features from the top of her head to the bottom of her feet. Leland rested easily on the bleachers, with his legs and arms crossed, but in his mind he could feel the shape of her body running beneath his hands. The soft wetness of her lips, the point of her chin, the length of her neck, the hard ridges of her ribs, and the gentle cushion of her belly. She was a new age girl with new age ideas, and she was by far his favorite.

Bridgett wasn't so bad either. Though her body tended to run more towards softness compared to Gretchen's, a little more cushion in all the right places. Not that it was a bad thing. Leland had nothing against a full-bodied woman. Even as he sat Leland could imagine himself holding her tight, her breath in his ear, his face buried in her long dark hair. But Mabel had been a full-bodied woman. Sometimes memories came back. Memories better left forgotten.

Leland took a flask out of his pocket, unscrewed the top and knocked back a swig. The moonshine burned in his throat. Gretchen gave him a dirty look and jogged his arm with her elbow.

"You should be careful with that."

Leland gave a derisive snort.

"Yeah, I can just see the headlines now. City Councilman Caught With Hooch. Judge Demands To Know the Source.

22

Hell, an article like that would probably beat out Babe Ruth Contract With Yankees Worth $70,000."

Gretchen's face didn't give an inch.

"I'm serious. You know I don't like it when you drink. A person of your standing should be acting as an example."

"C'mon Gretchen, a little drink every now and again never hurt anybody."

"But it's illegal."

Leland smiled and gestured farther down the bleachers where Deputy Johnson sat sneaking drinks from his own little flask. Gretchen's face was a mask of seriousness, but it quickly collapsed into tinkling laughter. She gave Leland a dirty look, took the flask from his hand, and took a pull. She coughed several times as she handed back the flask. It was strong stuff.

"You better put this away and pay attention. Your team is going out on the field."

She was right. Another out had come and gone while he wasn't paying attention and it was time to get back to work. Leland stuck his tongue out at Gretchen, grabbed his glove, and vaulted over the bench seat in front of him. Gretchen laughed at his antics.

"You are such a loony."

Leland turned his head back as he jogged out on the field.

"Only a quarter Looney."

He laughed and Gretchen laughed too. It was an old joke around town. Leland really was a Looney. His grandmother had been a Looney, one of the prominent early Oregon families. Leland could even remember his mother telling the joke when he was a child. The little woman laughing as she pronounced to the world that if she was willing to marry a man half Looney, what did that make her? For a woman who had grown up in a cabin with a dirt floor, she had a pretty good sense of humor.

The baseball diamond sat behind the high school with the outfield fence butting up against the hillside where kids and doctorates alike dug up rocks containing the imprints of long dead leaves and twigs. Two small nicely painted sets of bleachers sat on either side of the dirt diamond which got weeded every week by the club. It wasn't Ebbetts Field, but it looked pretty good for a little town of five hundred people in the wilderness of Eastern Oregon. Spike had called it quaint, but Spike had been living in Portland too long and gotten a bit of an attitude toward such things.

The weather was a little chilly. Leland wore his long underwear under his cotton uniform. It was a little early to start the baseball season, but the weather had been reasonably nice and everyone had been anxious to start playing again so the Fossil club and the Condon club had agreed to an exhibition game. It had been Leland's idea to use that word. It made the whole affair sound fancier than it was.

Leland started running for shortstop, but continued on to left field when he saw Tim standing there. Left field wasn't his usual position. He almost always played shortstop or at least one of the bases. Good grace kept him from ever saying it out loud, but Leland knew he was one of the better players on the team. But today that didn't matter. Today he had sacrificed himself to the back field so his brother would be allowed to play. Never mind that Willy couldn't play because his knee was still acting up from where a horse kicked him last month. The Condon club had been convinced he was trying to sneak in some big city ringer. Leland had assured them that Spike was quite the opposite, and then had thrown in himself playing the backfield to help sweeten the deal. Spike would have been just as happy to spend the afternoon at the house with his family, but their mother had been dead set against her sons not spending time together. It wasn't until Willy failed to show up that Leland had come up with the idea of his brother playing.

Spike stood out in right field, where he could cause the least amount of damage. He was tall and gawky, the opposite of

Leland's own bulky compact build, and looked entirely out of place. Where everyone else wore their matching cotton uniforms, he wore the trappings of an insurance salesman minus the tie and jacket, which Leland had made him take off. In all fairness Spike was an insurance salesman, but to have a suit in the latest cut seemed a little frivolous to Leland. Spike stood out in the grass, looking a little lost, repeatedly adjusting his ill-fitting borrowed glove, Leland's spare. Leland had big thick hands. Spike did not.

A batter walked into the box and Joe, Leland's best hand, leaned back and let fly with the first pitch. The bat swung, connected, and the ball went sailing up into the air. Higher and higher it went, up toward right field, a lazy pop fly, the easiest hit in the world to catch. Spike ran across the field to get underneath it. Leland watched the baseball drop down. Falling from the sky at a slower speed than it rose. Down came the ball, up came Spike's glove, and then the solid sound of the connect as the ball hit Spike right in the face.

Both teams and both bleachers burst into laughter at the sight of the former native son from Portland sprawled in his fancy clothes down in the dirt. Leland laughed along with the rest of them. The batter jogged around the bases and Spike sheepishly lifted himself up from the ground, picked up the ball, and threw it back to Joe at the pitcher's mound. Leland yelled across the field.

"Must be letting yourself get soft little brother. Must be all that easy living. Your wife must be treating you too well. I'll have to have a talk with her."

The team laughed once again and Spike glowered at his brother, one eye slowly swelling shut. Spike looked as though he would like to snap off a couple of comments toward Leland about wives, but he didn't. Their mother had raised him too well and there were certain things taboo. Instead he brushed off his nice clothes as best he could and went back to watching the next batter walk up to the plate.

Leland had never been shy about saying what he thought. Spike was cut from a different fabric. He'd always been a lot quieter, a lot more subdued. He rarely let it show when he was upset or displeased. Even when their father had decided that it would be best for his younger son to be sent to high school at a Portland boarding school, Spike never said a thing. Everyone in the family knew that he didn't want to go, that he'd rather go to the local high school like his older brother, but the old man's mind had been made up. Leland would have put up a fight. Spike just kept quiet all summer, packed his bags in the fall, and got on the train to Portland, never kicking up a fuss.

Lots of pitches, a couple hits, one strike-out, one easily caught fly ball, and one forced out at second. The inning ended with little fanfare and the Fossil club returned to their bleachers as the Condon club retook the field. Leland was first up. He picked up his favorite bat and sauntered out toward home plate, his cap set at a jaunty angle. Leland took a couple of practice swings, imagining each one connecting with the ball and sending it sailing over the fence to the hillside beyond. He eyed the opposing pitcher, a gangly kid who worked in Condon's mercantile, and stepped into the box.

The wood of the bat felt good in his hands. The pitcher eyed him like a coyote eyes a rabbit right before it springs. The first ball came in fast and low. Leland let it go by. It was a junk ball. There was no reason to swing at junk balls. Luckily the umpire agreed. You could never tell with local umpires, especially after all the drink they tended to get in themselves by the late innings. The second pitch came curving in like a snake. It was perfect, just where Leland wanted it. Leland swung his bat and connected heavily with the air. The ball sailed safely past. Strike one.

Leland stepped out of the box and shook his arms a little to loosen himself up. He stepped back into the box and the pitcher smiled like they were old friends. The pitcher's arm bent back and the ball came sailing in, a fastball, a little below dead center. Leland swung and the air was filled with the crack of the connection. The ball flew up into the sky, becoming just a dot lost in the blue, and came down straight into the waiting glove of the catcher behind him.

Leland cursed under his breath and walked back to his side's bleachers feeling dejected. The boys all looked disappointed and Gretchen's face was filled with empathy for how he felt. Joe handed him a flask and Leland sat down and took a drink. Leland was a solid hitter and it was rare that he didn't make it onto base. Leland sat in silence and watched the next batter take his own saunter out to the batter's box.

Leland took another drink from the flask, letting the warmth course through him, and handed it back to Joe. Tomorrow would be Monday and it would be the start of another busy week. Leland was always busy. There was the work on the family ranch, spread across the surrounding hills and canyons. That always kept him busy. There were several hired hands, but Leland liked the feel of sweat on his brow and the ache in his muscles when he went home in the evenings. The evenings were usually full as well. Board meetings for the bank, board meetings for the milling company, board meetings for the telephone company, and council meetings for the city. Then there were also his less official business interests, his hobbies, and his socializing.

It was all good work. Exciting work. Work where Leland knew everything he did helped better the place he loved. The place his father had helped create. Leland could look back over his forty years and think of not one moment he would rather be anywhere else than where he was now. God it was a beautiful day. This was the best place in Oregon, the best place in the country, the best place in the whole damn world. Leland was not a religious man, but he did thank god every Sunday that he had never had to go out looking to find his personal Elysium.

Spike got up from where he was sitting by himself, picked up a bat, and walked out toward the batter box. There were already two outs and Leland knew they'd be going back out to the field soon. At each of his previous times at bat Spike had unceremoniously been struck out. Each time, three pitches, three swings, then a lanky man walking back, eyes downcast and apologetic.

Spike didn't seem to understand what he was missing all around him. He hadn't wanted to go to Portland, but he sure as hell had taken to it like a fish to water. Leland was the eldest son, his place in the world had never been a question. When the old man had started to get sick it was Leland who had taken over, shouldering the load of his father's legacy. When the old man died it had been Leland everyone had looked to. It had never been a question of if, only of when. It was a lot of responsibility, but it was also freedom.

In Portland, Spike was nobody. Just some replaceable cog in a giant insurance corporation. A man of little consequence or bearing. In Fossil, Leland was an important somebody. A man about town who commanded respect and whose advice was often sought and whose opinion bore great weight. For Spike, the younger brother, it had never been an option. Their father had groomed Leland from the day he was born until the day the old man died. The heir to the throne. For Spike, their father did his best to find a place for his younger son. A future somewhere else so he didn't have to live in the shadow of his brother. In Leland's mind it was the best arrangement for all. Spike had never voiced displeasure. Even if he had, given his current position in Portland, Leland doubted Spike had the business sense to keep all the family's interests in line. Joe tapped him on the arm, breaking Leland from his thoughts.

"Do you want to head up to the still by Spray tonight? Kluff probably has another batch ready to bring down."

"Hell Joe, tonight? You know my brother is in town."

"I know, I ain't stupid, but I'll be damned if I know when the hell else we'll have a chance to get up there. You know how people get when they run short. Besides, we need the cash for the bulls."

Leland let his mind shift from baseball to the bigger picture. Joe was right. He was often right, it was what made him a good employee. They did need the money. Joe was supposed to board a train to Omaha on Wednesday. He was going to bring back some high end breeding stock, high quality bulls to breed with the rangy desert cows in the family herd. Better bulls would shift the family herd's reputation from scrub cattle to high end. It was something Leland had been wanting to do for a while, but it took a lot of money. The still had proven to be very effective at solving that problem, for the bulls and several other projects. It was important for the family. Spike and his mother would just have to understand.

"Yeah, come by the house after dinner and we'll head up. Be sure to bring some flashlights and a raincoat. It looks like it's going to…."

The connection of bat and ball sounded like a thunderclap. Leland looked up just in time to see the white orb sail over the center field fence, landing far up the hillside. Spike dropped the stake of wood out of his hands triumphantly. A flash of white teeth cracked his face and he began an easy victorious jog around the bases. The Fossil stands stood and began yelling and clapping, Leland amongst them. They were soon joined by polite clapping from the Condon side. Spike stepped on home plate and doffed his cap to the crowd before walking back to his seat. The Fossil club members crowded around him, shaking his hand and slapping his back. Leland waited until the group cleared a bit and then shook his brother's hand.

"Good hit little brother. One hell of a home run."

Spike smiled back.

"Thanks Leland."

The last few innings played out and the sun made a soft landing on the surrounding hills. The game ended with a score of three to three, not a win, but not a loss. The two teams shook hands and went their separate ways, little knots of men and women talking. Leland walked around to the front of the school with Spike and Gretchen. Leland helped Gretchen into his Model T and then turned to his brother.

"I need to take Gretchen home. Would you mind walking down to the house?"

Spike looked at the woman sitting in the car, looked at his brother, and shrugged his shoulders.

"Sure, no problem."

"Thanks, tell Mom I'll be around for dinner in just a bit."

Spike headed off down the hill and Leland climbed into the car next to Gretchen and hit the electric start. It was beginning to get chilly and the lithe woman snuggled up against him. Leland adjusted the side mirror, catching sight of his square jaw covered in stubble, put the car into gear, and headed down the hill into town. Gretchen lived on the north end with her elder sister. Together they ran a small boarding house for the local cowboys and lumbermen who periodically came into town. The pair rode in silence until Leland brought the car to a halt at the house's front gate.

"Thank you for the ride. I enjoyed watching the baseball game."

"Thank you for coming."

Gretchen started to get out but Leland grabbed her hand and pulled her back. He pulled her in close and kissed her on the mouth. She melted in his arms and returned his sign of affection. In his mind Leland could see someone coming upon them, the forty year old man and the twenty-five year old woman, carrying on like a couple of teenagers. The thought pleased him and he let it roll lazily through his head. One arm held her close and the other inched upwards from the curve of her hip to the rise of her breast. Gretchen pushed his hand down and pulled away.

"You are the devil."

Leland smiled like a naughty child caught with his hand in the cookie jar.

"Who me?"

Gretchen kept her face stern, but there were obvious cracks in the veneer. Her face was flushed and her eyes gave away what her other features would not.

"Have a good night Leland."

"You have a good night too. I'll see you on Friday."

"I'm looking forward to it."

"Me too."

Gretchen got out of the car and Leland watched her until she walked into the front door of her house. He put the car into gear and headed back down the darkened street. There was no light along the town's boulevards except for the muted glow from the houses. The stars shone overhead, bright flecks in the evening sky. The belt of the milky way arched across the heavens, slowly disappearing behind advancing legions of condensed moisture that promised future precipitation. It was all so beautiful. There was nowhere else he'd rather be. The bright lights and flashing bulbs of Portland held no interest for him. What were the constructs of man compared to this? Mabel had never felt the same way. She was more drawn to the world built by hands rather than the cathedral wrought by nature. She had never been happy out in the middle of nowhere. She had never understood. For her, the descriptions had been better than the reality.

Leland concentrated on the street outside the windshield. It was not worth thinking about. It was not worth remembering.

Some things in life could not be changed. Things were better without her than they had been with her. She had been holding him back. Keeping him down. He doubted he would be half the man he was if she had stuck around.

The car pulled into the driveway next to the house that Leland shared with his mother and two children. It had been his father's house before his. It was a big house, meant to hold a large family. Most of it was empty. Leland got out and walked around the back to the kitchen, dragging his feet on the mat before he went inside. The kitchen was warm and filled with the smell of the recently prepared meal. Leland stood and let the smells waft around him. Taking a final breath he pushed his way through the swinging door to the dining room beyond.

Leland's tiny mother sat at the center of the table, passing portions to those around her. Spike and his loving little wife with the short hair sat opposite her, watching over their two young boys, neither older than five. Robert and Cynthia, Leland's children, sat on either side of their grandmother. All of the children sat in silence. Spike's children due to discipline, and Leland's due to personal choice. Both Robert and Cynthia had reached the age where words were used sparingly, and usually just for requests. There was nothing wrong with that. Leland could remember himself during that age. His mother had done a good job in raising them. They were courteous and polite, kept up their studies, and rarely got in trouble. In truth Leland preferred their current state of sullen silence over the constant prattle of their past selves.

Both of his children made Leland feel uncomfortable. Interactions with them were always clouded by old memories and pains. Both of the children had the look of Mabel about them, especially the girl. When he looked at them he could see Mabel's face as she made him breakfast that last morning. The creases on her brow and the downturned angle to her mouth. It was her eyes that he most remembered. They seemed to sparkle and to be full of life again. He could remember a feeling of elation that morning from seeing her eyes like that. The first day of spring after a long cold winter. Perhaps things were finally getting better. When he got back that evening she was gone.

"You're late." Leland's mother's voice did not match her stature. It resounded around the room.

"I had to take Gretchen home."

The old woman looked displeased, but she kept her opinions to herself. She always did. Leland never raised his voice, he didn't smoke, he was a good provider, and he never drank to excess. It was an unvoiced truce that allowed Leland amnesty for his vices. The old woman knew about the needs of men, and could see no reason to deny her eldest son the comforts that his transgressions provided. Such things were not for her to judge, reserved for a higher power.

Leland sat at the head of the table and the small talk began again, flowing around him as he sat in silence. A plate covered in beef, potatoes, and canned greens was pushed toward him, but he politely set them down and selected an orange from the bowl of fruit on the table, a rare treat brought by Spike from Portland. He wasn't very hungry. His mother gave him another look, but again, it was not her place to question. He rolled the orange between the table and his palm, listening as Spike told the story of his home run. Leland added quick witted quips of his own from time to time, pinches of pepper on a bland meal.

As Spike shifted to the latest happenings in Portland and the trials and tribulations of the insurance industry, Leland bit the orange peel and his mouth filled with the taste of bitterness. He kept silent as his brother prattled on, their mother listening with adoration and Spike's little wife's eyes filled with devotion. Leland ran his thumb along the wound, separating the peel from the golden fruit beneath. The orange was not ripe enough. The peel did not come off easily and it left behind a thick layer of white.

Spike droned on and everyone sat politely and listened. Leland tried to pull the orange apart but it resisted his will and the wedges refused to separate in the neat way that nature intended. Juice was dribbling on the table and Leland felt a gentle hand upon his arm. He looked up and Spike's wife, smiling sweetly, handed him a napkin. Leland returned a weak smile and took the napkin to clean up the mess. The orange was ruined. Too much expected of it before it was ready. Leland wrapped the remains in the napkin and set it to the side next to his untouched plate of food.

The clock chimed and Leland excused himself from the table. Joe would soon be arriving and he needed to change clothes. Spike and his mother both gave him looks as he rose, his mother disapproval, his brother curiosity. As he left the dining room and mounted the stair, he could hear Spike ask for a second helping. Off came the baseball uniform. On went work pants and a work shirt. Leland heard a knock on the front door and rushed down to open it, getting there just ahead of his mother. It was Joe. A few polite greetings and a refused offer to come in. Leland grabbed his overcoat and hat and followed Joe outside. As he shut the door he turned back to his mother.

"I'll be back in the morning."

His mother said nothing. It was raining outside, a solid rain that gave promise of harder blows before the night was through. Water was rapidly filling all the ditches, inconvenient miniature rivers destroying the villages of mice and the kingdoms of ants. Leland stopped for a second at the thought. It was something his favorite professor from university used to say. An old gray man as dusty as his books, talking with great sweeps of his arms before a sea of young faces glowing with limitless possibilities and a lack of responsibility. Funny the things that stick in a mind. The two men got into Joe's waiting car and they drove off out of town. Joe's fingers fidgeted on the steering wheel.

"Hell of a shift of weather."

"Yep."

"Do you want to wait and do this another night?"

"No, too much stuff to do. I wouldn't have time until next week and that would be too late. Let's just get it done. If it rains too hard it probably won't last long."

The car bumped up the road, climbing up into the hills and timber. With each bump the beams of the headlights flickered, went dark, and then blazed back to their former glory.

"What's up with your headlights?"

"I don't know. Something wrong with the fuse I'm guessing. Haven't had time to take a look at it."

The two men rode in silence. The car climbed to the top of the hills and then dropped back down the other side where it began to follow the winding course of the river. The river was high, fed by mountain snows assaulted by the early spring. Leland stared out through the windshield, alone in his own head. The car crashed through puddles and the rain fell harder. The men's breath steamed and the inside of the windshield began to fog up. Both men intermittently leaned forward to rub it clear with the sleeves of their overcoats. Joe cursed the rain under his breath.

"Maybe we should just give it up tonight. This storm is looking pretty bad."

"C'mon Joe, we've already made it this far. Besides, you can see the lights of Spray up ahead. We'll stop at Johnson's for a little while and let this storm pass before we head up to Kluff's."

Joe was silent but he put more pressure on the accelerator, looking forward to being somewhere more warm and dry than his old car. He turned his head toward Leland and the car hit another pothole, splashing water up along its sides. The headlights flickered and went out and Joe cursed and fiddled with the knob. The lights came back on with sudden clarity, illuminating the edge of the road and the river in front of the car.

"Watch where the hell you're......"

Leland grabbed for the steering wheel. Joe seemed frozen with fear. The car bounced as it went over the bank and in. The car began to tip and sink as soon as it hit the river. The water was cold and swift, icy claws reaching up to draw them down. The sudden shock prodded them into action. The two men swiftly worked themselves out of the sinking car.

"Jesus Christ," yelled Leland.

"We're going to have to swim to shore," yelled Joe.

"No shit. Only one problem, you know I can't swim!"

It was dark but Joe could see how pale Leland was. The two men shivered as the sinking car was dragged farther out into the river. The shore was only fifteen feet away.

"No problem. Just grab onto my coat tails and kick as hard as you can!"

Leland didn't want to go into the water. He could already feel it pulling around his legs as the car sank. But what choice did he have. It had to be done.

"Okay!"

Joe leapt forward and Leland leapt after him, his hands frantically grabbing for the thick fabric of his friend's overcoat. The icy cold of the water hit him like a sledge hammer, driving all of the air from his lungs and ebbing away the feeling in his fingers. Joe dog paddled toward the shore and Leland held grimly on, kicking his legs as hard as he could. Twelve feet to go. Leland could feel the swift undertow of the river try to pull him down to the depths below. Ten feet, nine feet from the shore. Joe's kicking feet battered his face, striking his nose and forehead, but Leland would not let go.

They were getting swept farther down the river. Eight feet, seven feet, six feet. An image of him and Joe at the upcoming dance telling a story about their current predicament flashed through Leland's head. Friends and neighbors laughing and clapping him on the back. Gretchen holding him close as they danced. His mother fussing over him when he got home. Five feet more. Leland's hands were cold, his feet were cold, his entire body was cold. He had never before felt so cold. He could feel his grip loosening. He could feel his hands slipping. He could feel the river start to take him.

Four feet. Joe put down his legs, his feet touching the sandy bottom. He pushed himself forward into shallower water. The weight on his coat suddenly lifted and he turned to see Leland swept back out into the maelstrom, his hands clawing wildly for the coat that was no longer there. Joe screamed but dared not throw himself back into the watery hell from which he had just escaped.

Leland fought and struggled as the river dragged him away from the shore, his limbs transformed themselves to lead and all feeling left his body. The river sucked him under and he felt the coldness sap away, disappear as his body was overwhelmed. His mind screamed out in anger and terror, struggling to regain control of a body that would no longer listen to its commands. He had too many responsibilities to die like this. Too many things to do. Too many things to take care of. Leland felt water fill his mouth. His mind seemed to go numb and like his body ceased to struggle. He was in the iron grip of a giant, a force he could not fight. The dark watery world around him began to fade. An entire life played out before him in just a second, a life never in his control, and froze on Spike's cocky grin and blackened eye as he slowly jogged around the bases. Leland smiled. Everything was going to be okay.

A Late Night Conversation

"I miss her."

"Shut up."

"I do though."

"I don't want to go through all this again. She's a bitch."

"Don't say that. I still love her."

"That's pretty stupid. What's done is done. It's time to move on."

"I know. But it still hurts."

"Look, I miss her too. I miss the conversations we used to have. But she made her decision and it's time to move on. There's lots of others out there."

"I miss lying next to her, that feeling of serenity. That feeling of caring for someone and knowing that they cared for you. That feeling that this person can accept you for everything you are."

"I don't want to do this again. She treated both of us like shit."

"It's not her fault."

"Yeah, then whose fault is it?"

"I don't know."

"That doesn't help me understand."

"I don't understand either."

"You know she has demons."

"She's become our demon. Every time I try to move on you jerk me around. Every time I try to think about something else you want to talk about her. I'm getting sick of it."

"You know you still think about her."

"I don't like problems without solutions. Things without logic."

"So you think it's better to just bottle everything up inside and never talk about it?"

"Yes."

"I don't. I've done that before, I've closed myself off from the world. It hurt. I'm not going to do it again."

"Is this any better?"

"No. Why do you think it hurts so bad?"

"Because you opened yourself up and held nothing back. Because you loved her and she did not love you."

"I thought she loved me."

"Even if she did she obviously doesn't care two shits about you now. You've become a nuisance, a pain in the ass."

"She can't even understand why this hurts to bad, can she?"

"No, she can't. She feels no empathy because she's never felt this way. It's like a toddler running around hitting people because they have no idea what they're doing is hurting people. Then one day somebody hits them and they understand that it hurts."

"I wish we could help her."

"There's nothing we can do."

"I know."

"It's time to move on. Staying here does nothing."

"You're not the only one giving advice like that you know."

"Who else?"

"You know who. He says it's time to move on. Time to not give a shit. He says we should just go and look after ourselves. Conquer one after another, regardless of what we have to do to get it done."

"That sounds like really bad advice."

"Just because we don't plan on staying doesn't mean we couldn't care about them while we're there."

"You'd still be most likely hurting them. You'd be no better than her. I wouldn't listen to any of his advice. He doesn't care about anyone but himself. He's a dick."

"Do you think that……?"

"I don't want to talk about it anymore."

"But…."

"No."

"Do you think we're ready to move on?"

"I don't know."

"How will we know?"

"I guess it will stop hurting."

"What if it doesn't?"

"I don't know."

"You remember the dream I always used to have?"

"No."

"I used to have a dream where I'd be with a woman. Going through our day to day activities, making love, holding each other. It always felt so serene, so at peace, so good. But every time I woke up I could no longer remember what the woman looked like."

"So?"

"I still have that dream, but now it's her. She's made my favorite dream into a nightmare."

"I don't know what to say. I have no control over that."

"Where do you think things went wrong?"

"We both know the answer to that."

"I don't."

"I think things went wrong from the start. A relationship with that many rules will never go well. She obviously had problems that she was not willing to talk about."

"Why couldn't she talk about them?"

"I don't know."

"I would have loved her no matter what."

"I know."

"It makes me sad, sad for her. Sad to know that she'll never find what she's looking for if she never opens up."

"There's nothing we can do. Besides, she had no right to treat us like she did. We're the victim. We're the ones who got jerked around. We're the ones who got ground down to nothing. All those days of wondering if today would be a good day or a bad day. All those days of watching her pick us apart. All those days of waiting for her to open up. She was the one who failed."

"She was scared, you could see it in her eyes. You could tell that she didn't like what was happening either."

"We tried everything we could think of. But when someone isn't even willing to tell you what the problem is, it's impossible to solve it. She ground down our confidence until there was none left. She destroyed the very things that made her attracted to us in the first place, and then broke up with us because they were gone."

"It hurt, watching the distance grow each day. Watching her get further out of reach."

"It's her own damn fault. It was a relief to finally just let her end it, to stop fighting it."

"It didn't help for long, did it?"

"No. Too many loose ends. Too many unanswered questions. Too much pain. We gave up so much for her. We had a pretty good thing going before her. We were happy. She had no right to take that away."

"It's my fault. At the time it seemed that if she could be that interested in us, that it must be something worth checking out."

"I went along with it. I didn't try to stop it. We both should have known better. What kind of person can pursue you while you're boning their cousin? It's all pretty fucked up. Sometimes I miss that, miss those moments with her cousin. Enjoying each other while keeping that distance, so neither one of us could get hurt."

"It's never that simple."

"I know."

"The cousin was the one we originally pursued in the first place, remember?"

"Yeah. But if she ever wanted more, she never said anything. I'm not a fucking mind reader."

"People rarely say what they're thinking."

"Yeah. I used to worry that the whole cousin thing would be what ruined it with her."

"Maybe it was part of it."

"Who knows?"

"She does."

"That doesn't help."

"Do you think we could ever go back to how things were before?"

"I doubt it. We can't really do anything until we get over her. I don't want what happened to be an excuse to hurt other people."

"Maybe it would help us get over her."

"What would we talk about? How some selfish bitch crushed us down to nothing? I'm sure women are just lining up to hear about that."

"Take it easy. I'm trying to be positive."

"I know. I'm sorry. This is why I didn't want to talk about it."

"I wish that we had never left on that trip. That's where the trouble seemed to start. It was afterward that everything seemed to go from being fun to work."

"What happened while we were gone wasn't her fault."

"Parts were. I should have been mad, but I was just glad that she was all right. It could have been far worse."

"We should have quit then, when we first got back and she first tried to break up."

"Why didn't you?"

"I let you talk me into fighting it. You were in love."

"She let you talk her out of it twice. She cared. She wanted it to work."

"Yeah, but love takes work. When only one person is working at it and the other is just sitting there waiting for a miracle, things break. That's the part that hurts. Having her agree to keep trying, and then have her not try at all. All it did was make the breakup easier on her, gave her more time to let go. It only got harder for us, the more effort we put in, the harder it got. She's a selfish bitch."

"She probably feels differently about it."

"Probably, no one ever thinks of themselves as a piece of shit."

"You know about her anxiety."

"I hated that word, anxiety, it became an excuse. To sit there and say you have anxiety, but never say anything else, to never really talk about it. What did she expect to happen? The only person who won't collapse under that strain over time is someone who doesn't care. She ground both of us down to

44

nothing, until we were no longer what she loved, so she could have an excuse for what she did."

"She was scared. She wants to find love, but she doesn't know how."

"The way she acts she doesn't deserve love. I hope that someday someone hurts her just as badly as she hurt us."

"You know you don't want to see her hurt."

"I know."

"Remember how you scared her, how defensive she got when we were angry, when she wouldn't tell you why she broke up with us."

"I still feel bad about that."

"If only she would have just used words instead of silence. There is nothing she could have said that would have made us stop loving her. Even if things ended the same way, at least we would have understood. There wouldn't be so much emptiness."

"We both tried telling her that. She doesn't care. She only gets mad because we can't be as dead inside as her. She wants to shut herself away so that she doesn't have to feel any hurt. She doesn't want to have to face things that she did. She saves herself from being hurt by hurting us twice as much. Fucking bitch."

"Stop calling her things like that. It doesn't help anything."

"It makes me feel better."

"But not for very long."

"Yeah."

"She wants to be friends."

"Why should we bother?"

"It would make things easier. We're stuck in the same social circles. You don't want to lose those too, do you?"

"She's done nothing to act like a friend."

"You could just pretend."

"We've been hurt worse than we ever have been before. I'm not going to pretend nothing happened. I'm not going to pretend like she's not a bitch. You were the one telling me not to hold things inside. If she wants to be friends so bad then she should make the effort. She should say the things she couldn't while we were dating."

"Do you think she ever will?"

"I try not to hold out hope for such things. We have to move on."

"I know. But how do we do it?"

"I don't know."

"They say that it just takes time."

"That's bullshit. It's already been longer than we were actually with her."

"So why do we still hurt?"

"Because we invested a lot into it. Can we please talk about something else?"

"I don't know what else to talk about."

"We might as well try to be happy with what we've got."

"I'll try."

"I will too. Good night."

"Good night."

The Care Package

Larry Hunt opened his door and walked into the brisk morning air. The trees on his block were vibrant. Reds, yellows, and oranges, far outnumbering the few patches of green that remained. Fallen leaves lay scattered across the yards and sidewalks. The day was chilly, not yet cold, but definitely a noticeable difference from the high heat of the summer months.

Larry shivered and zipped up his fleece. The hair on the back of his arms clung to the sleeves as his arms moved beneath them. The air was dry, full of electricity and static.

Larry shivered again and clutched the envelope more tightly against his body. The letter-sized envelope was yellow and heavy duty, a forever stamp graced by Madame Curie stuck to its upper right corner. A clumsily written address, scrawled as if by the wrong hand, stretched across the center. No return address. The envelope could not come back.

Larry stepped off his stoop and began his eight block walk to the mailbox. The weight of the envelope was both a comfort and a curse. There was no way he could lose track of such a hefty envelope. It was a solid weight in his hand. He held the envelope so tight that its edge pushed into his palm. It felt far heavier than the thirty notes inside.

The morning sun peeked through the branches overhead, its blinding light intermittently shaded by the trees that grew along the street. Oaks, elms, maples. They all provided the same comfort. The same sense of not being trapped in a world of concrete and cruelty. Sidewalks that would have once been flat when built now rose up like rolling hills in a meadow. The concrete pushed heavenward by the slow and tireless heaving of the roots beneath. It was a quiet morning. Few people around. No one to watch his sojourn. No one to see him shake, pulsed by tiny vibrations of anxiety.

"Of course it has to be cash, you damn fool. Do you think these are the kind of people who want you to send a cashier's check or your credit card information? They want you to know nothing about them and for them to know nothing about you. That's how these things work."

Teddy's tone had been akin to lecturing a small child on the realities of the universe. Teddy, a long time drinking buddy who enjoyed Miller Lite in tall boy cans. Teddy, a Dale Earnhardt look alike who would be unnoticeable if he didn't look so out of place everywhere he went. Teddy, the man who knew how to take care of things when things needed to get done.

Larry shifted his focus back to the world around him. He couldn't let himself do that. He couldn't let himself think too much about what he was doing. It was crazy. It was absurd. If he thought too much about it he would probably lose his nerve.

He would probably turn around and walk back to his house, and that would solve nothing. It was better to distract himself. Better to catalog and analyze the world around him, rather than the memories and thoughts inside his head.

Old Mr. Cavanaugh labored in his front lawn, raking up the few leaves that had already fallen. The old man had worked in a factory back when people still worked in factories. He had put in his time and finally retired on the insistence of his wife. Old man Cavanaugh had once said he considered it the biggest mistake of his life. He had been working his entire life. It had not made sense to quit just because his time on this world was growing late. The old man stopped his early morning raking just long enough to wave hello to Larry and exchange pleasantries. Larry returned them, but did not stop walking. He did not want Cavanaugh to see the cold beads of sweat that covered his brow.

Life had been simpler in the Navy. They told you to get up, you got up. They told you to eat, you ate. They told you to shit, you shit. Every part of a person's life had been directed, out of their control. Every minute was timed and planned. One did not have to think in the Navy. As long as one got their work done in a timely and satisfactory manner, one was free to do whatever one wanted. As long as whatever one wanted was exactly what their superiors wanted them to do. There had been something comforting about having absolutely no control. Something nice about being a single cog in a much larger organism. Larry missed the Navy. Larry wished he had stayed in like some of his friends had. But that time had come and gone. The greatest comforts had seemed like the worst prisons at the time. Larry shook his head as he walked. There was no use in dwelling on things three years in the past.

Cross a street. Turn and look both ways. Childhood drills that never really go away. There were no cars. No one in their right mind would be moving so early on a Sunday morning. The neighborhood would soon come alive. People walking in their Sunday best, the smell of frying bacon, the laughter and pounding feet of children as they rushed down stairways. Soon the neighborhood would be like an old Folger's commercial. But not yet. At that moment all was quiet. Just the soft breeze moving tree branches like the skeletal hands of death rubbing together in anticipation. The tinkling of wind chimes played a sad melody in the cool crisp air.

"This has to be taken care of. This is not something that can be ignored." Teddy had been most insistent, and he was right. This was something that could not be ignored. "I'll take care of this. I know some people, people back east, people who know about garbage."

There was no doubt that Teddy did. Teddy knew about these things. Teddy knew people. Teddy was quiet about his work. He rarely talked about it unless coaxed with friendly words and offers to buy a couple more rounds. Larry had heard him talk about work only a few times during the long years of their friendship. Teddy worked for himself, but himself worked for the government.

"Like a contractor, you know, someone who knows how to get in touch with the right people to get your house built."

Another street. Larry started across. Before his first step hit the ground he heard the frantic ringing of a bell and an adolescent bellow of warning. Adrenaline rush. Larry raised his head and dodged as a bike whizzed past down the street. Its rider, a pinched faced twelve year old, his local team baseball cap worn backward and a large bag of Sunday papers hanging from his shoulder. The boy turned to curse at Larry as he sped past, but once he got a clear look the boy's eyes widened and he turned back, his mouth still closed, and rode off down the street. Larry did not recognize him. He was not the neighborhood's paperboy. Probably just passing through on his way to his own delivery area. Larry settled his breathing, let his beating heart slow, and continued walking toward his goal. How had he let himself get so distracted? He needed to keep himself focused. He needed to keep his mind clear.

"Be sure to take care of Amy. Always watch out for Amy."

That is what Larry imagined his mother would have told him, if she could have before she slipped away forever. It had been his mother's mantra when he was a child, beaten into him by its repetitiveness. His mother had been gone for two years, but it still drummed inside his head.

"Protect. You must protect your sweet innocent sister."

It was like an order from a C.O. It was not something that he could question. It was a fact of life. It didn't matter that Amy wasn't really sweet or innocent. He had been born the older brother and that's what older brothers did.

Amy had always been a stubborn child. No one could ever tell her what to do or how to live. It took all of their mother's strength just to force her through college so she could have a real job, a real life, not be like their mother. Amy looked nothing like their mother. Their mother had been dark haired, short, homely, quiet, and subdued. Amy was blonde, tall, loud, and undoubtedly a looker. There was one thing she had in common with their mother. She was undeniably attracted to douchebags and assholes. The lineup of boyfriends Larry remembered from their time in high school were all the same. Kids who thought they were big shit because they had nice cars and nice clothes. The kind of guys who wrapped their arms around a woman like they were giving her a headlock. The kind of guys who thought they were the center of the world.

It was too bad. Amy had been a sweet girl. Obnoxious at times, but caring. She had always just wanted someone to care back. Larry cared, and their mother had cared, but it wasn't what she was looking for. Larry could understand. There was a difference when the person wasn't obligated. That had always been their mother's problem. It had to have been hard for her, and lonely, raising two kids on her own. She had done the best she could, but had always craved what she had been denied. Their mother had been desperate to be in love. Amy never had a good role model.

When Larry came back from the Navy to live with and take care of their mother, he had discovered that Amy hadn't really changed. Yes, she had grown into a beautiful and confident woman. Yes, she had a good job at a marketing firm. Yes, she had a nice car. Yes, she had a fancy apartment in a posh neighborhood. But the douchebags still remained. A reminder that perhaps it was all a just a veneer surface. Proof of the cracks that still existed in her psyche.

A car drove slowly up the street from behind him. For the briefest of moments Larry had an uncomfortable feeling that the driver was watching him, following him. He refused to turn his head to look behind him. He was just being paranoid. Nobody could know. Nobody had any idea. Well, nobody but Teddy, but Teddy could be trusted. The car drove by up the street, neither speeding up or slowing down. A dusty blue four door Hyundai Excel, a fat middle-aged black woman at the wheel in a Sunday dress and hat. Larry chuckled to himself and his own paranoia, but he quickened his pace as he crossed another street.

Soon his chore would be done. He just needed to hold himself together and control his thoughts for a little bit more. Larry tried not to dwell on the delivery of his envelope. He tried not to think too hard about what it contained. One step after another. Each bringing him one step closer. Study the cracks on the sidewalk, watch the clouds blow across a slowly brightening sky, think about the breakfast that he would make when he got back home. Eggs, sausage, pancakes, and a big glass of orange juice. It all flitted through Larry's mind in the blink of an eye. Look at the world. Think about whatever you want. Just don't think about what you're doing.

"Everything will be taken care of, don't worry about it, there's nothing to worry about."

Teddy had told him that so many times that he had actually started believing it. He had never liked Nick. There was something about him that just made you instantly dislike him. Something in your subconscious, something from the ancestral days on the savannah, that just told you to beware of that kind of person. Amy had been dating Nick for a year. From the very first time Nick had shook his hand, squeezing harder than Larry just to show he could, Larry had known that Nick was nothing but trouble.

Nick was an ex-Marine, not big, but imposing. He was a good looking guy. His haircut remained in the classic jarhead shave. He tended to wear sports jackets over tight jeans and a tight shirt. There was something in the way he moved, something that went beyond being sure of yourself to being cocky about yourself. He was tall and handsome. When he talked to you he had the uncomfortable trait of staring you right in the eye, never averting his gaze. He made Larry uncomfortable as hell. He made Amy swoon.

Larry had tried to like Nick. He had tried for Amy's sake. He just couldn't get himself to do it. There was just something off about the guy. Larry had followed his gut. He had done some checking with some old friends that were still in the military. The prognosis had not been good. Nick had gone into the Marines because he had been a troublemaker. He'd hung out with the wrong crowd, been involved in drug using and dealing. Nick had continued to get into trouble several more times while he was in the service. Larry had tried to tell Amy. She had just laughed, pulling her hair away from her face in that way she always did. Nick had told her all about it. Nick was a changed man. Larry had gotten in plenty of trouble when he was younger, but it didn't mean he was a bad guy.

Larry tried to like Nick again. He told himself that Amy was right, people did change. Larry was not the same person he once was. Nick had gone into the Marines for many of the same reasons Larry had gone into the Navy. Larry tried having more one on one time with Nick. Tried to get to know him better. He had even taken him out for drinks one time with Teddy. Teddy had hung around for only half an hour before excusing himself to go home. The next time Larry saw Teddy the statement had been short and to the point.

"You need to get rid of that guy."

A blue bird flew in front of Larry, startling him out of the depths of his mind. It rushed by in a flash of blue and landed on a low branch not far ahead, bursting out a harsh chirp to greet the morning, chastising him for walking around at such an early hour. Larry stared at the bird as he walked by, studied its plumage, examined every facet and detail as though he was trying to commit everything to memory. The bluebird studied him back, but did not find him near as interesting, so flew off. The bluebird was safe. The bluebird was good. The bluebird was not something Larry was afraid to think about. He wished it had stayed.

He hadn't been there when it had happened. He might not even have known about it if it hadn't been for Amy's roommate Leslie. She was a perky simple redhead who worked as a secretary at the same marketing firm as Amy. She had seen all of it. She had seen Nick and Amy arguing. Leslie had watched Nick get more and more frustrated at Amy. She had heard him raise his voice time and time again. She wasn't sure where the tipping point had been. She was walking back from the bathroom when she saw Nick grab Amy by the arm and Amy shake him off. Then the punch, straight to the face, Amy on the floor, Leslie and the other patrons in stunned silence. Nick left. Amy and Leslie took a taxi home. A week later Leslie had called Larry. She was worried.

Larry had tried to talk to Amy. The things she said had scared the shit out of him. She was not leaving Nick. He had been under a lot of pressure. He'd been really stressed out. It was partially her fault. These things happen. He felt terrible about what had happened. It would never happen again. Excuses, excuses, excuses. Just like their mother used to make for their father before he finally left them forever to go spread misery elsewhere. Larry hadn't known what to do. Amy wouldn't listen to reason. Nick was a Marine, an imposing burly Marine. There was no way Larry could kick Nick's ass.

Teddy had known what to do. Teddy didn't even hesitate in bringing it up as soon as he heard the story. "There's ways to take care of these things." Teddy had told him what to do as they sat at Larry's dead mother's kitchen table, sipping tall boys. "These things can be taken care of. You don't want to throw your own life away for some piece of trash. Garbage men clean up the trash. That's why we have garbage men."

Houses gave way to businesses, their doors and windows locked, slumbering until the start of the day. The big blue mailbox sat on the corner. Larry opened the hatch. He held the envelope in his hand, but couldn't push it forward. It was absurd. The whole thing was crazy, sending the envelope through the mail. Larry felt the envelope with his hand. He could picture the contents in his mind. Three thousand dollars in cash, a picture, and a typed noted describing home address and favorite haunts. How could anyone fail to recognize what was in the envelope? How could anyone picking it up not know? The contents felt so obvious to him.

None of it made any sense. This didn't seem like the kind of thing you could just mail off for, like the decoder rings from the back of his childhood comic books. It all seemed too simple, too out in the open. Could this really be how it was done? Was there really some box in some post office where things like this were sent? Did some innocuous looking man come in to check the box every day, walking past unknowing patrons shipping packages and buying stamps? What about the name on the envelope? Surely it wasn't a real name, but could a fake person get a post office box? Was nobody checking? Was nobody watching?

The envelope was in Larry's hand, poised upon the brink. Maybe all his doubts were just in his head. Maybe his anxiety was just getting the better of him. Maybe the contents of the envelope were obvious to him just because he knew what was in it. Maybe this was the way things were done, right out in the open, just under everybody's collective noses. It really didn't matter. Larry didn't have a choice. He could turn around, walk back to his house, and nothing would get done. But then what?

Larry pushed the precious envelope down into the dark depths of the mailbox. It fell to the bottom with a satisfying clunk. Its contents were out of his hands. Larry felt great weight lift from his shoulders. Whatever else happened now, it was out of his control.

Junipers

It was a simple device, but effective. A handle attached to a steel can, a long spout with a wick on the end. You fill the can with diesel and light the wick on fire. Tip the can and out pours fire. The trees were dry, their once dark green needles turning brown in the cold dry December air. They burned easily. Men had come amongst them, men with chainsaws and heavy machinery. One by one the tall majestic trees had been ripped from the ground, their gnarled roots exposed to the open sky. It was a declaration of war. The end of a slow retreat. It was an act of genocide. None had been spared upon the rugged hillside. Giant old trees, aged fifty years or more. Young trees, barely just saplings. It did not matter, all were ripped from the ground by the excavator and unceremoniously left to die, slowly starving from the lack of water and nutrients.

The junipers had been there for as long as the son could remember, but they had not always been there. Old photos, grainy black and white images from a century ago, gave proof to their slow invasion. The junipers had always crowded the hillsides, even in the earliest of his memories, but once the hillsides had been bare. The junipers have but one natural enemy. Fire. Fire brought to earth by lightning strikes, fire that spreads across the hillsides and canyons, burning everything that stands in its way. In the old days the junipers hid amongst the rimrocks, hiding in the one place where they could be safe from the unholy light and heat. Any juniper that dared to grow away from these sanctuaries would find itself consumed by the next burning blaze.

Then came the Europeans, who built cities, roads, and towns. Who brought grains to grow in the rich soil and livestock to graze the thick bunchgrass. They saw the fire and they feared it, for it consumed their labors as easily as it consumed the junipers. The Europeans fought the fires, they brought forth the power of science and technology and they conquered the devouring element. They threw it back whenever it appeared and defeated it before it could spread across the land.

For every action there are benefits and consequences. The Europeans beat back the fire and benefited greatly from not having to fear its wrath. However, the junipers did not need to fear the fire anymore either. Slowly the junipers began to emerge from their rocky sanctuaries. At first one or two appeared. Moving off the bluffs. Taking root in the canyons and valleys below. One or two became three or four, three or four became six or eight. Generation by generation the junipers marched forth into the lowlands, an unstoppable conquering army.

It was a gradual invasion, one hardly noticeable within the perception of time held by mere humans. A steady advance over one hundred and twenty years. It was a devastating invasion. The junipers sank their roots in deep and drew to themselves all of the nutrients and water around them. The junipers would allow no competition for the valuable resources they needed. Springs dried up, their water stolen before it could reach the surface. Other plants, bunchgrass and sagebrush, withered before the onslaught.

The past is full of mistakes, and the present and future are full of trying to fix them. The lords and ladies of the state government saw the problems that the juniper invasion had brought. They created grants and pledged money. A declaration of war was made. The hillside had once been covered by the dark green of the junipers. Now all that remains are the brown corpses, victims of the dendrocide.

The father and the son silently fill the cans they carry with diesel and light the wicks with matches from a small metal cylinder the father always carries in his pocket. Their breath steams before them, hot exhales attacking the cold December air. The cloudless sky is a great blue dome above their heads. Their booted feet crunch in a few inches of snow as they walk up the hillside. The son's breath becomes labored as he moves upward, it's hard work in his thick warm clothes, carrying the heavy can. The father and son did not carry out this massacre. A man had come with an excavator, he had done the slaughter. Their duty is of a different sort. Someone has to dispose of the corpses.

They move within the shattered grove. Around them are fallen giants, once standing proud and tall, now brought low and laying on their sides. Their roots claw like arthritic fingers at the sky, small patches of dark dirt still clinging desperately to them. Each of the hasbeen conquerors has been conquered themselves. When the father and son reach the top of the hill the father points and each go to opposite ends of the once proud grove. For a moment, as the son steps away, the anguish returns and he begins to feel his eyes grow misty. He chokes the emotions back. He pushes it down deep inside of himself. He concentrates on his work.

The needles of the juniper before him have mostly turned brown. They are lifeless. They make the perfect kindling. The son tips the can and the diesel pours through the spout and through the wick. Out of the end comes liquid fire, splashing onto the dry needles and branches. The fire ignites quickly and spreads with a crackling roar. The can tips a few more times over other spots. It does not take long, at first the fire is small, a few minute flames creating a menorah on a few delicate branches. Within minutes the tree is engulfed in a fiery storm. Flames leap upward twenty feet. Furnace like heat pushes the son and the snow away from the conflagration. A great column of black smoke reaches upward, a single finger stretching for the heavens. The monster is dead, but its passing has been marked by a funeral pyre worthy of a Viking king.

It's glorious to see. There's something about fire, something about staring at it that entraps the mind. Fire is a friend, it provides warmth and comfort. Fire is an enemy, it destroys wantonly and without remorse. Fire is chaotic and magical, it flickers and dances to a beat only it can hear. Fire cleanses all. Where once lay giant trees, within a few hours will only be heaps of gray ash. The son wishes that the fire could cleanse him, destroy the deadwood that has fallen upon his soul.

The son looks away from the hypnotic flames and moves to the next fallen tree. He repeats the process again, committing another tree to a fiery end. One eye is on what he is doing, the other keeps track of where his father is. They both move back and forth across the hillside, lighting trees as they go, keeping parallel to one another. If the son gets too far ahead he stops and waits for the father to catch up. If the father gets too far ahead he stops and waits for the son. Several times the son's wick goes out and he walks over to light it again off of his father's. Less often the father walks over to relight his wick off of the son's. The cans are finicky. Pour too slowly and only small bits of fire drop onto the tree, swiftly burning out. Pour too quickly and the diesel drowns the wick. The son understands the science behind it, but it's still annoying to have a so called flammable liquid put out a fire.

It's an easy job, simple motions. Walk up to the tree, light it on fire, make sure it's going to burn, if not light more of it on fire, walk away. With the first few you have to concentrate on your work, make sure you're doing everything right. After that it becomes automatic, your body doing the job without direction, freeing your mind to wander. The son sees her staring at him, pain and longing in her eyes. Pain from the hard struggle, from fighting a monster that neither one of them understand. Longing, wishing for things to be the way they once were, for the world to be filled again with the hope that this time, this time, the monster would not come back. The son's brain is going full bore. Desperately trying to figure everything out. Desperately trying to put all of the pieces of the puzzle together. Desperately trying to still save the day. Her eyes, the saddest eyes the son had ever seen, glint with unwept tears.

"I don't know what to do. I don't know what to do."

The son's words fill the empty December air, a flat slow whisper amongst the crackle of the flames. Hot tears run down his cheeks. The smoke must be stinging his eyes.

A sudden updraft of fire throws itself skyward. The son jumps back and moves quickly away from the searing heat, rubbing his hand across his eyebrows to make sure they're still in place. Now is not the time to doze off. This is not a job you can do in autopilot. The flames are not to be trusted. The son sees his father a little further down the hill, waiting for him to catch up. The son wipes his eyes with the back of his hand and then hurries forward, lighting trees as he moves farther down the hill. Back and forth, back and forth, none are spared, and none will be left to rot. Finally both the father and the son reach the bottom of the hill. There are no more junipers left to burn. They put down their cans and take off their jackets, laying them on the ground to sit on so their butts won't get wet in the snow. They relax and watch the wonders of their own creation.

Ninety fires burn above them. Ninety great columns of black smoke reaching upward into the air. Dark pillars holding up the sky. The trees on the upper end are burning much slower now, their branches and needles all scorched away. The trees lower down the hill still throw great arms of flame up into the sky, fiery infernos for which the devil himself would be proud. It's an amazing sight, ninety islands of fire, kept separate by the wet ground and snow. It's a strange feeling to see them burn, to see all of the waste. Junipers do not make good lumber, their trunks are too crooked, too filled with knots. No one would ever use all that could be offered. Junipers do make good firewood, they warm the house the son grew up in every winter. But again, the supply is too much for the demand. The father and son do what has to be done. The good is greater than the bad.

Even the majesty of the natural world can only distract a man from his inner turmoil for so long. As the father and son sit and watch the son feels his view turn inward again. The burning pyres before him become nothing but background to the storm that blows within him. It's all so fresh and raw. Memories of joy, memories of sadness, of pain, desperation, confusion. Not knowing what to do. Not knowing how to let go. Not knowing why. The son's eyes fill with tears. He tries to hold them back, but the dam has been broken. He does not sob, he does not convulse, he only loses control of his eyes. Tears run down his cheeks. The father looks at him and the son turns his head away to hide his shame. The father looks back at the fires above and waits.

The father is a quiet man. He does not talk a lot, does not feel the need to fill the air with sound. He is friendly and cordial when people are around, always quick with a joke, but the life he has chosen has left him with a lot of time alone. Isolated with nothing but his own thoughts. Life on a cattle ranch means that you are always busy, but so much of the work requires only your feet and hands, not your mind. The son considers the father a wise man. The father watches all of the world, takes it all in, accepts it all as it is. He has gained his wisdom from experience, from having lots of time to think about the world, and from not forgetting the lessons he has learned or the lessons others have learned around him.

The son has rarely asked his father for advice. There is some kind of fierce pride within the son that makes him want to prove that he can do everything on his own, that he doesn't need anyone else. The son has become full of grief and heartache, sadness and despair. He is full to bursting. He is on fire. It has to be let out. He can't contain the pain anymore. At first he talks in broken sentences, long pauses as he tries to put things together in his head. Slowly it gains steam and begins to take on a life of its own. The safety valves burst open and everything that has happened with her over the past few months spills out. It comes like a torrent. The story skips around, and in the rush to get it out parts are missed then gone back to. The son's soul vomits at their feet. He has never spoken to his father about these kinds of things before. The son looks at the ground, ashamed to look up, distraught at his outburst of humanity. In a soft voice he whispers his mantra.

"I don't know what to do."

The father is silent, his gaze watching the son steadily as the bile and pain streams forth. When the son finishes he looks away up at the hillside. In his eyes the son can see the hurt of past memories and the pain of an inability to stop the hurting of one's child. The empty void in the son fills him with desperation. He needs something to fill it. Some answer to the questions that torment his mind.

"Why is she doing this?"

"Because she's scared. She's scared and confused. Just like you."

The two sit in silence, watching the deadwood burning before them. Evidence of their power and might. They have the power to shape and alter the world around them, but not take away the burdens of themselves or others. After a little while the father rises, picks up his coat and his can, and walks back to the pickup. The son sits for a little longer, then rises and follows, carrying his own coat and can. It's time to go home.

A Memory That Just Popped In My Head

When I was growing up we lived in a very remote area. I mean really remote. The closest town with any amenities was twenty-three miles away and it goes without saying that for a large part of my formative years the only kids I saw on a regular basis, outside of school, were just my two brothers. Growing up this way never seemed weird to me. It was just how things were. To a child, any situation they find themselves in is normal, and assumed to be the same for everybody. Nothing is weird until it's pointed out as being weird.

I got my first bike when I was five or six. The exact tracking of your life on a timeline just isn't that important when you're that young. I imagine maybe we didn't have a lot of money at the time, but for whatever reason I did not get a new bike. My parents instead gave me an old bike that had been at my grandmothers. Though the bike was old, it was probably built back in the 1960's, it was in good condition and a little tuning by my Dad made it just as good as any new bike. I never noticed that it wasn't new, since to a kid, it doesn't really matter if something is old as long as it works just as well. Please note, if your child does care about this at age five, you're probably not raising them right. Not judging, just saying.

Anyway, I loved the shit out of that bike. This was the bike that I started out on training wheels with, riding around the driveway. This was the bike where I learned that even with training wheels you could get in some pretty gnarly wrecks. One of my favorite memories was hitting a rock so hard that it popped one training wheel up higher than the other. Instead of fixing it I just rode it around that way, happily throwing my weight back and forth, rocking the bike from one training wheel to the other.

It was on this bike that my parents taught me how to ride using just my own balance. It was on this bike that I learned that sometimes your parents will lie to you (i.e. "Don't worry, I won't let go."), but that they were only doing it for my own good. That bike opened up a whole world of exploration for me. Suddenly I could travel by myself just as far as my legs were willing to take me. My life had all new adventures. My bike was my motorcycle, my Star Wars speeder bike, my valiant steed carrying me into battle, and even sometimes just a bicycle.

I rode that bike for several years. I can still picture every detail of it in my mind's eye. The handlebars swept out high and back like the antlers on a proud elk. The long banana seat, its color faded from long use, a curved metal bar at its back. I never had to worry about racking my nuts on the crossbar because it curved downward and allowed for easy mounting and dismounting. The chain guard was a faded pink that matched the color of the seat. My description may have led some of you to notice a single problem with my bike. I did not notice the problem until I was about eight and some of my older brother's friends came for a sleepover. They promptly pointed out I was riding a girl's bike.

In retrospect it did have *Wild Flower* written on the chain guard.

Heroes

Growing up I always read books about heroes. People who rode forth to do battle not for glory, not for money, but because it was the right thing to do. People who fought for an ideal, for the betterment of those around them. These heroes had doubts, these heroes had flaws, but they always managed to rise above it all. They always managed to conquer their own fears, and in the end, to do something bigger than themselves.

I always wanted to be a hero. I always wanted to be that person on the white steed. Saving those who could not save themselves. Facing down challenges and sacrificing myself so others could continue their lives and be happy. Being a hero means you must make sacrifices. I always told myself that if the opportunity ever came that I would make those sacrifices. I would do whatever needed to be done to ensure the best for those I fought for. Those I cared about.

In the books the heroes are always celebrated. Whether they stay and gain all that they have ever wanted, ride off into the sunset, or make the ultimate sacrifice, the hero is always loved. It is easy to want to be a hero when you base all that it means off the words that are written in a book. On those pages everything always turns out for the best. The ending is always happy. The hero, no matter how low they are brought, always rises back to glory. The books do not talk about what happens when the hero loses. What happens when the sacrifice is made and nothing comes of it. The books don't talk about the damage done to the hero.

Major Wilkins Comes Homes

Major Wilkins lives in a nondescript two bedroom house on the middle of the street with his wife and two daughters. If you were walking to his house you would pass under rows of oak trees, old but neatly trimmed. You would walk past rows of identical houses, all built to the same specification. The same corner window, the same flat board siding, the same one car garage. Major Wilkins' house is yellow with brown trim and a red door. To the left is an identical twin, only painted blue with white trim and a white door. To the right is a second identical house, only painted white with green trim and a green door. The white house always looks dingy, probably because it is white.

Major Wilkins' house always has a neatly cut and well watered lawn and well kept bushes and flower beds. His wife likes to keep a tidy home. The flower beds have daffodils, violets, azaleas, and one large rose bush at the corner of the house. A short cement stair goes up two steps to the front door. An American flag hangs next to the door. Major Wilkins has one of the best kept houses on the block.

The inside of the house is nice, clean, and orderly. The floors are hardwood. The hardwood floors are covered by ornate rugs, some of which the Major had sent home while he was touring overseas. The furniture is all heavy and good quality, either family heirlooms or purchased from a furniture dealer. None of it is the cheap shoddy furniture that people buy from department stores. The walls are elegant shades of tan and light brown. Pictures hang from the walls. Family pictures, pictures of beloved ancestors, and even a few paintings by somewhat known local artists. Everything is kept in its place. The Major's wife sees to that.

Major Wilkins is a career military man. He has been in the military since he was eighteen. He started as an enlisted man, but went through officer training when he decided that he did not want to leave the army. Every day he wakes up, gets in his mid-sized sedan car, and drives out to the nearby military base where he is in charge of procurement and supply. He would prefer to be in charge of something else. He feels that his talents are being wasted, but he does his job well. All of his superiors tell him this, and he has received several commendations for his excellent work.

Every day after work Major Wilkins goes to the officers' club and has a few drinks with several of his friends, some of whom he served with overseas. They like to sit and talk about their lives as military men and their past tours of duty. Every day he leaves the officers' club promptly at 6:30 PM and then drives home to have dinner with his family. Major Wilkins is a family man. He goes to church with them every Sunday and always attends his children's school events. He is always the first to stand for the pledge of allegiance or national anthem.

Major Wilkins is well liked. All of the people he works with, whether they are subordinates or superiors, respect him. The soldiers that work under him could not have been treated better by their own parents. He is calm and patient with them. He always takes the time to help them become better soldiers. He is always ready to offer a helping hand, or an ear to hear their problems and worries. The Major cares deeply for his soldiers.

Major Wilkins is a veteran. He has served three tours overseas. If it was not for his injury he would have volunteered for a fourth. He cannot go on a fourth tour. His leg is wounded and did not heal correctly. He has a slight limp from the injury, a slight limp that is just enough to keep him home while others are shipped out to foreign shores. The Major does not believe this is fair. He does not believe his injury is significant enough to keep him in procurement and supply stateside. But Major Wilkins is a good soldier and does what he is ordered to do without question.

Major Wilkins is a war hero. If you saw him in his dress uniform you would see a row of campaign buttons, two Silver Stars, and a Purple Heart. When the Major was fighting overseas, anytime they needed a volunteer, he would step forward. He did not do it out of a sense of pride or duty. He did it because he loved the men he served with, and knew that by putting himself in harm's way he kept them out of it.

The Major's first Silver Star was awarded when a convoy he was escorting came under attack. The road was mined and the lead Humvee was destroyed, effectively creating a roadblock. Gunfire from an enemy strongpoint raked up and down the convoy, wounding several fellow soldiers. The Major did not hesitate, he attacked the strong point with rifle fire and grenades, advancing over open ground. The enemy retreated and the convoy was saved.

Major Wilkins' second Silver Star was awarded when a detachment he was leading came under heavy enemy fire. The detachment set up a strong point in a building but in the rush to find cover two wounded men were left behind. The Major ran from cover into the open and helped one of the wounded soldiers hobble back to the building. He then ran from cover a second time, under heavy enemy fire, and carried the second wounded soldier back to safety. It was while carrying the second soldier that the Major was hit several times in the leg, earning him the Purple Heart as well as an unwanted free trip back stateside.

Major Wilkins is a great man. Pretty much everybody thinks so. His eldest daughter, Lucy, does not think so. She thinks he's a bastard. She wishes that he had died that day overseas. Before the words are even fully out of her mouth a hard slap knocks Lucy to the floor. Her nose is bleeding. Her red cheek is pressed against the hardwood. She looks over and sees her little sister cowering in her mother's arms. She meets her mother's eyes, but her mother looks away, comforting little sister.

It's hard to say what set him off. There seems to be little pattern or reason behind it. Sometimes it's because something is not put away properly. Maybe the salt was left out, or maybe toys weren't put away after play time. Major Wilkins likes to have a neat and clutter free home. Sometimes his family does not meet his expectations. Sometimes something isn't as clean as it should be. Sometimes the children are too noisy or the television is on too loud while he is trying to read. Major Wilkins dislikes having to repeat himself, and he rarely has to. Major Wilkins' family lives in fear.

Lucy rarely forgets herself. She is twelve. She knows how to avoid the Major's wrath. She knows how to tell when he should be avoided, when it is all right to play, and when she should just sit quietly in her room. Like her mother she has learned how to survive. The Major's youngest daughter is only seven. She is still young. Sometimes she forgets herself. Sometimes she forgets the world she lives in.

Little sister was playing too loudly before dinner. She was running around the house screaming like a banshee. Little sister was being a seven year old. Major Wilkins was trying to read a book. He was trying to relax before dinner. He has not had a good day. Several of his subordinates caused screw ups that had taken the whole day to fix. His leg is aching especially badly this evening, a constant annoyance and reminder. He is drunk. The conversation at the officers' club had been lively, and because the day had been more difficult than normal, he had partaken in two extra gin and tonics. His temper flared and he put his book down. He got up to discipline his daughter the only way he knows how. The same way he was.

Major Wilkins grabbed little sister by the arm and gave her a shake. He chastised her, shook her more, chastised more, his voice growing louder. Lucy knows what is coming. She won't let it happen. She steps in between her father and her sister. She pushes him away from her. Her little sister rushes to her mother who is standing in the doorway. Mother crouches to hold little sister. Lucy pushes Major Wilkins and yells at him to leave little sister alone. The Major's flaring temper turns into a fiery rage. The backhanded slap that throws her to the floor could have leveled a grown man.

Lucy stares at her mother who will not look her in the eye. Why won't she do anything? Why does she do nothing to protect her own children? There is a monster in the house, but mother just turns away as though not seeing it makes it not exist. Two little girls. Two little girls she brought into the world with the monster, and she is powerless to do anything for them. Her ability to fight has been sapped long ago. Lucy feels anger at her mother's inability to save her. Hatred at her mother's cowardice and fear. There is also pity. She knows why her mother cowers and hides. She has seen her mother get worse.

The first kick to Lucy's stomach knocks all of the wind out of her. It's like a dump truck hitting her. The blood that falls from Lucy's nose onto the rug further enrages the Major. Lucy refuses to make a sound or let him see her cry. She looks at her little sister. The little girl holding tightly to her mother, head buried in her mother's bosom. Still believing that the woman holding her can offer any kind of protection. Lucy's little sister is precious. Her little sister still has a chance. Lucy doesn't have a chance. She has lived too long in a world that does not make any sense. She is too damaged. She is old enough to know that too much hurt has been done. That even if her father died the scars would not heal. She cannot be fixed.

But little sister, she can still be saved. She is young. She still has a chance to someday have a normal life. That's why Lucy got in the Major's way. That is why she always gets in his way. The second kick takes her in the diaphragm, right below the rib cage. A wail escapes her lips and tears involuntarily pour down her face. Lucy had tried to wrap herself into a ball, but she wasn't quick enough this time.

As her vision clears she stares upward at the house's living room ceiling. She refuses to call the house her home. A home is a safe place. The ceiling is painted white and is textured. Her eyes travel across the ceiling and down the tan wall to an old black and white picture of the Major's great grandparents. They stare back solemnly and unsmiling. Lucy remembers back when the monster was gone overseas. A happy time. A good time. A time of laughter and love. Most people wish the war had never started. Lucy had prayed that it would never end. Her tear filled eyes continue searching around the room, finally falling on the Major, his face contorted, silent in his rage. Lucy stares at the man she will never call her father. The third kick catches her below the belly. Bile fills her mouth. Her bowels spasm. She feels the dank greasy stickiness as she shits herself.

Thirty seconds. Only thirty seconds from the slap until the Major's rage is subdued. He stalks out of the room. The front door opens and closes. The Major takes a walk like he always does when he loses his temper. Lucy rolls on the floor moaning. Her body tightened into a ball she cannot relax. Tears flow down her face. Her mother waits until the monster is gone. Waiting until she's sure it's safe before coming over to comfort her eldest daughter.

Memory

It's interesting the things we can remember over a long period of time. The details that stand out sharp while others fade away. There seems to be no rhyme or reason to it. I have an excellent memory. I remember much more than other people. Most of the memories normally remain hidden, but with the right stimuli great details can be brought forth, like films loaded into a projector for viewing. Entire conversations, sights, sounds, tastes, touch, and emotions, all brought forth by a single stimulus, a single memory. Once one memory is remembered it triggers more. A cascade of recollections with which, if I so desired, I could explore the entirety of my life. Every piece of elation, shame, anger, happiness, and sadness laid bare for my mind to see.

The earliest memory that I have must be from when I was about eighteen months old. There are no pictures of the event and I'm the only one who remembers it. It's so vivid in my mind, as though I never left that moment in time. It's a warm summer day. My older brother and I are sitting in the grass in a shady corner where the porch and the house come together, hiding from the brightness of the sun.

"Your name is Shawn."

"Sawn."

"No, no. Not Sawn. Shawn."

"Sawn."

My brother says the word slower, his mouth moving with great care to enunciate every movement of lip and tongue. The hiss of the shh sound is like a leak in an air hose.

"Shhhaaawwwwnnn."

I can still feel my frustration. My anger at not being able to make the word sound like he does. I watch every movement his mouth does closely, noting every detail, but there is some secret to it that is escaping me. Some hidden movement that I am not capable of. I try with great care but only meet with more failure.

"Sssaaawwwn."

My brother shakes his head at me and I begin to have a fit. The frustration overwhelming my brain's ability to function past primal urges and basic emotions. My mother comes out and takes us both inside for a snack. Graham crackers, we had graham crackers and grape Kool Aid. I don't like grape Kool Aid. Another disappointment.

I often imagine my memory as being like a giant cavernous library, filled with everything I have ever learned or experienced. When my mind is focused it's an incredible tool. I rush down the stacks, knowing exactly what I'm looking for. Digging up facts and figures for my use. My memory makes me extremely good at my chosen profession. I forget nothing that I take in. All of the pieces can be easily gathered and put together to complete the puzzle.

When my mind is idle it changes from someone rushing through the stacks looking for a particular reference to someone wandering around, taking random books off of the shelves. Sometimes only reading the back of the book to get a general idea of what it's about. Sometimes opening the book to a random page to read a few specific passages. As my mind focuses more and more on a specific memory, more and more details come to the surface. It's like traveling back in time. At first parts are blurry, but the more I focus my mind the more clear things become. I'm certainly not a Rain Man, memorizing everything people say, though I do remember many conversations in their entirety. My ability to recall is dependent upon how interested I am in the stimuli. I'm not going to remember what somebody was wearing, unless I took special notice of it in the first place.

People often wish for better memories. They wish they could sit and remember all of their happiest moments. Have every thought, feeling, and emotion painstakingly recorded so they could bring them out and smile when they are feeling blue. Having too good of a memory is terrible. We are meant to forget. Yes, we lose the overwhelming emotion of our happiest times, until the memories seem as faded photographs against the brilliance of reality, but not all of our times our happy. Feelings evoked by incidents are meant to become watered down by time. For every good memory there are also bad ones. Memories that we would rather not forget, the loss of our happiest moments, are a small price to pay for relief from the torturous pain of the bad parts of our lives. Our very sanity depends upon it. I have an exceedingly good memory.

An Awkward Black History Month

It had been a fun evening, but as they all do, it had come to an end and it was time to return home. As I walked through the underground parking garage a wave of contentment carried my tired body and mind forward. Good friends, excellent conversation, and three pina coladas were soon to give way to my nice warm bed. I smiled to myself as I thought of my peaceful safe haven just fifteen minutes away.

Each footstep echoed through the confines of the garage, bouncing off of the low ceiling covered in pipes and signs warning about the low ceiling and pipes. The garage was quiet, no other soul but myself in sight. The rows of parked cars, endless upon my arrival, now had their numbers cut in half.

Some of the cars, like mine, had yet to be claimed by people heading home that night. Others would be left to slumber in the world of concrete, their owners unable to reclaim them until the morning sun brought clarity of thoughts and actions.

My feet carried me past car after car, different makes and models, varying colors, their backs all gleaming beneath bright fluorescent light. Their fronts hidden in shadows and darkness. Up ahead I could see my own gallant steed, a bright blue Ford Focus. Not a pretty steed, but reliable. One that would soon be carrying me home to a world of dreams.

The click of a car door opening was like thunder through the silent garage. My car's dome light turned on, a lighthouse beacon across a concrete sea. This was a problem. I heard these sounds and saw that light while still being twenty yards from my car. The shadowy figure moving between my car and the one next to it was not me.

I have often thought to myself what I would do in these situations. While sitting around bored my brain would often concoct complicated scenarios and the appropriate actions to take if I ever found myself in them. A thief is robbing your car in a deserted parking garage. Walk calmly by and pretend you don't notice them. Pretend that your car is farther down the line. Pretend that the nice man totally has some kind of legitimate reason for breaking into what is obviously his own car. Once out of sight call the police. This is why you pay a hefty premium every six months for car insurance. There is no logical reason to take any other course of action.

Of course, in the real moment, I do none of these things. No, instead my blood heats up and my fists clench. My brain forgets logic is a thing. Instead it shoots straight to *no rotten mother fucker is going to rob my car* mode. Never mind that there is nothing of value in my car, that the most a thief will get is my stock radio and a used ice scraper with brush attachment. No, my brain skips past all of these rational thoughts and goes straight to *you're going down mother fucker*. My body puffs up like a cobra, trying to make itself as intimidating as possible. My footsteps quicken as I break into a fast walk to cover the distance.

Now many people will probably think this about the stupidest possible way to react to catching somebody breaking into your car, and they are absolutely right. However, even in my idiocy not all logic and reason abandoned me that night. As my feet ate up the distance between me and my car a very simple, primal, and stupid plan formed in my head. Confront the robber and scare the shit out of him. If he has a knife, gun, or is even just a big mother fucker, run like hell. Again, a very stupid plan, but I was a little caught up in the moment.

I round the car next to mine. The thief is bent over next to the open driver side door, his head and shoulders inside, rustling around. My voice booms across the garage with authority.

"What the hell do you think you're doing?!"

The would be thief pulls his head out of the car and looks up at me, his eyes filled with shock and surprise. His back begins to straighten. Everything begins to move in slow motion.

My eyes and mind work in conjunction, quickly taking in every detail of the suddenly slowed down scene. The thief is a black man in his mid-twenties, he's of average height with a slight build. He's wearing a striped polo shirt tucked into a pair of dockers, both one size too big for him. He has a large afro and a neatly trimmed goatee. I can see both his hands. Both are empty. No place to conceal a weapon. That's good. His eyes are filled with surprise and a trace of fear, caught in the act. The car is unharmed, no broken windows, no obvious signs of forced entry. Fluorescent light reflects off the car's blue paint and custom rims.

My brain, moving at top speed, suddenly hits the brakes. Custom rims? Who the hell puts custom rims on a 2006 Ford Focus? My mind desperately tries to jerk me into another gear, forgetting to use the clutch in its hurry to catch the rest of me up with the situation. My car does not have custom rims. I am not standing next to my car. This confused looking man is not robbing my car. This......oh shit. My head turns and I see a second blue Ford Focus parked six spaces down. I look again at the poor shocked motorist before me. My body deflates. My face turns red with embarrassment. My eyes fall to the floor in shame. My mouth stammers, its boom gone.

"I'm...I'm so sorry, I thought this was my car."

The man gives me a look which conveys his thoughts of *what the hell man*? A look that quickly turns to one of sour reproach and disgust at the ways of the world and how a nice young man can't even get out of his car without some crazy white guy assuming he's robbing it. In my head I desperately try to come up with some way to convey the fullness of my regret for the mistake. Some way to convey that I'm not a racist bastard and that this terrible mistake has nothing to do with the color of his skin. My brain fails miserably, so instead I turn and walk away very quickly.

Art

Attraction is a lot like art. You can walk through the museum and look at all of the pieces. You can stop and appreciate each for its beauty and uniqueness. You can feel all of the emotion that has been put into it. You can recognize all of the qualities that make it great art. You may even stop for a bit and really try to look at it, really try to understand it. But then you turn a corner and there is a piece of art which you just can't look away from. You find yourself enraptured by it. There is something about it that sets it apart from all the rest. Other people walk by, to them it's just another piece of art, but there is something about it that speaks to your soul. Your eyes pick out every detail and the more you look the more you see. The more you see, the more you want to look. Before you know it you've spent an hour staring at one painting.

My Guide To Initial Messages While Online Dating Part 1

Eventually you hit the point where you accept that you're going to have to try online dating. You've tried everything else, and though the entire world seems filled with sexy singles, none of them seem to be in much of a hurry to beat down your door. The wells that have long sustained you, shared activities and friends of friends, have all run dry. The time has come, you see no other choice, and so you take the leap into the world wide web.

It goes without saying that I'm not a charming man. If I was a charming man, backed by the confidence that only comes from years of success or a narcissistic tendency, I wouldn't need to go trawling online. I'd just walk up to any woman that caught my eye and start a conversation. At least that's what I tell myself. Of course none of it really matters. I'm not a charming man, but there's lots of not charming men, and they all seem to be able to find somebody. So why not me?

The online dating world is frightening by its sheer scale. Tens of thousands of profiles representing people within just a few miles of you. It's stressful. First you have to write your own profile and pick out pictures that you feel best represent you. Then you have to sort through the tens of thousands of profiles to find someone you might like. Then when you finally find such a person you have to somehow gain their attention. Your initial message has to be funny, but not weird; succinct, but detailed; well written, but casual; and charming, but not creepy. It's a bit of an art. Below are my unedited attempts.

Attempt #1: 12Birds29

The first time always makes you nervous. You really have no idea what you're doing, but you try your damndest to keep anyone else from knowing it. The first profile I picked was that of 12Birds29, who judging by her pictures was some kind of an artist. Here's a woman, I thought, that would understand my sensitive side. Someone who would look at the world and describe it in the magical terms that were swiftly slipping away from my aging conscious. I saw no reason to beat around the bush. I just put it all out there for her to see.

I've always found people with artistic skills fascinating. It's probably because no matter how hard I try I've never had the skill to create in any medium what I see in my head, which I find frustrating. I have however, slowly over time taught myself to take photos, mostly landscapes, and have had some some people complement my them. Though my photos seem more like recognizing an opportunity when I see it rather then any kind of artistic talent.

I'd like to say up front that I really don't feel like my profile represents me as well as it could, though I'm not entirely sure how to correct this, yet. There's a lot of different facets to me and it takes time to reveal all of them.

All that being said I'm sending this because you seem like you'd be an interesting person to talk to and get to know. I imagine you get a lot of messages so I should probably write something enticing or witty, but I'm fairly tired right now and nothing is coming to mind. I could probably force something, but it would mostly just be bullshit.

Anyways, if you have any interest in getting to know me better, message me back.

P.S. How far can a dog run into the woods?

Was it successful? Of course not. I'm not sure what I was thinking. Especially the riddle. Why the hell would I add a riddle to the end? Who does that? Never mind the fact that I'm apparently terrible at spelling and grammar. The whole thing makes me cringe just reading it again. Then again, maybe I'm wrong about the whole situation. Maybe 12Birds29 never got back to me because her mind was too absorbed by the convoluted twists and turns of my riddle. Yeah, that was probably it.

Attempt #2: ChemicalKat

Okay, the first time didn't go so well. Obviously there was room for improvement. For instance, it would probably help if I brought up some things to possibly talk about. Maybe something from their profile, you know, so they would know I had actually bothered to read it. Also, it probably wouldn't hurt to do some proofreading before sending the message out. It sure as hell couldn't hurt. The quest began again. I sifted through countless photos and profiles to find someone who looked interesting, hunting desperately for something which might light a loquacious spark. Flying cars. ChemicalKat's profile included a snide remark about the lack of flying cars.

I am severely disappointed in the total lack of flying cars. I feel like this is something we were promised the 21st century would have, and that science and industry just let us down. Don't get me wrong, I do love many of our achievements, but c'mon, flying cars.

One of my favorite book series is the Mars Trilogy by Kim Stanley Robinson which outlines the colonization and terraforming of Mars. If I had a chance to join some kind of Mars colonization effort, I would do it in a heartbeat. Keeping my fingers crossed on that one.

It seemed like such an obvious step from one to another. Flying cars belong to the world of science fiction. Why not mention your favorite science fiction series? I'll tell you why, because it didn't work. I heard nothing back.

Attempt #3: RosewaterLips
Sometimes profiles have a strong pull in the physical department, but upon reading, they raise all sorts of red flags. At first you try to excuse it with the idea that they probably just have a weird sense of humor, but that nagging feeling doesn't go away. I don't know, the whole thing is pretty damn subjective. Such is the dilemma I had upon reading RosewaterLips' profile which proudly proclaimed that first, she wasn't on meth or

something; second, she would only date someone who could tread water longer than them; and third, she was a badass knitter. Let's be honest. It wasn't really a dilemma. I'm pretty weird myself, so I shouldn't really judge. Plus she was pretty hot.

Congratulations for not being on meth or something. That overall seems like a positive.

I can tread water for 30 minutes, would this be long enough to be competitive or should I start some kind of water treading training program with a Rockyesque montage?

Also, knitting is pretty good, but crocheting is more bad ass. Not judging, just saying.

Believe it or not, it worked. The dating world is strange in that you never know what's going to end up attracting somebody to you, but alas, sometimes the rocket engines light, but nothing happens. We messaged back and forth a few times and then RosewaterLips disappeared back into the electronic ether. Vanishing in all but my mind where she treads water and knits forever.

Attempt #4: FoxyHound32
Sometimes there's a profile that just doesn't have much of a hook. Either they haven't written that much, there just isn't anything to latch onto, or perhaps you're just getting lazy. Most of the time you move on from these profiles, but sometimes you still send a message, throwing out an inadequate piece of bait on the off chance that somebody calling themselves FoxyHound32 might bite.

This is probably a horrible way to start a conversation, but I'm wondering what makes your dog so special and unique? Looks like your everyday Aussie Shepherd/Blue Heeler mix to me.

I never got to find out what made that damn dog so special. My bait must have not been that good, because FoxyHound32 swam by with no interest. Looking back, it probably wasn't the best idea to start off by putting somebody on the defensive. Especially if the topic was her dog, which judging by how she went on and on about it in her profile, she would have probably married if it was legal.

Attempt #5: Dinomite69

Dinomite69's profile included some wisecrack comparing her iPhone to using carrier pigeons. At last, I thought, somebody that shares my proclivity for inane topics of conversation. Perhaps I had finally found my soul mate. Sure there were a few problems. For instance, like half the women on the dating site, she felt the need to point out on her profile that she had a very unique laugh. In my experience, using such descriptors as unique is often just a cover word for annoying as hell. However, nobody is perfect, so with reckless abandon I made my initial thrust in the swordplay known as online dating.

I really think you should reconsider carrier pigeon based communication. What a carrier pigeon loses in speed it more then makes up for by being a green technology. Just imagine a world where instead of showing off your new iPhone or Android, you show off your new speckled red crested pigeon, you'll be the envy of all your friends. Plus you get the two side benefits of entering your pigeon in the lucrative Chinese pigeon races (yes, this is a real thing), and putting Pigeon Fancier (one who trains pigeons) on your resume. Really seems like a no brainer to me.

Not to get off the topic of pigeons, but I was wondering what makes your laugh so unique and noticeable? Is it one of those tinkling of heavenly bells laughs, or are we talking about one of those Santa Claus has had way too much eggnog belly laughs? Both are fine, just curious.

Dinomite69 probably got too excited about buying carrier pigeons to have time to respond. At least that's what I tell myself. Besides, while carrier pigeons have many advantages over iPhones, they lack reliable internet connection. It was probably impossible for her to get a hold of me after she made the transition.

Attempt #6: LunaGirl

LunaGirl's profile talked a lot for some reason about how her favorite color was green. I'm not really sure why she felt such a thing was pertinent for a dating profile, but perhaps there was some kind of backstory involving true love only severed by a prospective mates' irrational hatred of the color. I don't know. Either way, there wasn't really all that much else in her profile. Under normal conditions I would've probably moved on, but for whatever reason I took it as a personal challenge. After all, if there's one thing I don't lack, it's creativity. To help things along, I made up a friend in a little white lie. This is of course not to say that I don't have friends, just that I don't have any who have a lot of interest in the color spectrum.

What about teal? I only ask because a friend and I recently got into a debate over whether teal was a shade of green or a shade of blue. Not to put pressure on you, but your profile does suggest you're some kind of green expert, and there may be a substantial bet of $5 riding on the answer.

95

It worked. It always helps to get people talking about what they know. However, it didn't really go anywhere. It's a little hard to branch out into wider conversation when the only thing you have to start with is a couple of odd comments concerning the color green.

Attempt #7: Skirtsahoy
I will say that I'm pretty sure I was slightly drunk or something when I wrote this next initial message. It was not the best of times. I was starting to get frustrated with the whole online dating thing. It was actually quite a bit of work, what with sorting through profiles and trying to decide what the hell to write. Is it any wonder then that eventually one shifted into the zone of being completely bonkers?

So, when you say you enjoy scaring the crap out of yourself while watching horror movies, do you mean that figuratively or literally? I'm only asking because I recently got a new Ikea couch (note the subtle hint that I have exquisite taste in furniture) and there is only so many times you can flip a cushion. Plus getting out to Ikea just to buy new cushion covers is a bit of a pain in the ass; what with the drive, the meatballs, etc. Now there are always exceptions, but in general I'd say I consider defecating on my furniture a deal breaker.

However, I really have no problem with you peeing and throwing up on yourself while riding a roller coaster. I'm fairly classy and wouldn't even do the whole pretend I don't know you thing. Nope, I'd walk proud with you through the amusement park for the rest of the day. Though I'd probably leave my window down on the car ride home.

For the safety of my furniture and car seats it's probably better that someone who stated that they like to scare the crap out of themselves while watching scary movies and pee themselves on roller coasters did not respond back. I'm not really sure what I would've done if she had.

Attempt #8: BailaSalsa

You get to see all types while perusing online dating profiles, and one must always be ready to use whatever opening they can to try and get their message to pop up above the crowd. However, one must always remember that it's a fine line between playfully poking fun at someone, and actively making fun of them. BailaSalsa's profile gave the impression that she had a fascination with the movie *Clue*, which is fair, give that *Clue* is awesome, what with its multiple endings and all. However, it also mentioned that her high school class had voted her most likely to go skydiving. She was twenty-seven. It goes without saying that I did not put a lot of effort into this one.

Sure you were voted most likely to go sky diving, but did you actually do it?

I'm fully with you on Clue being a great movie, one of the more under appreciated ones in my opinion. Which was your favorite ending?

I don't know much about flirting with the fairer sex, but I do know that pointing out someone's flaws is probably not the best way to get them to talk to you. But then again, if they're bragging about being voted most likely to go skydiving in high school, and then never do it, they probably don't have good follow through anyway.

Attempt #9: Cakesfen

Cakesfen's profile seemed to suggest that she really enjoyed running and drinking. Of course I had to introduce her to the idea of the Hash House Harriers, the infamous drinking club with a running problem. It was a perfect opening, or at least it would've been if I hadn't gone on from there deep into crazy town.

Sometimes when I'm using this thing I get an uncomfortable sensation that OkCupid is far too similar to buying a car stereo off of Amazon. Really all its missing is just a section for comments from other people who have tried the "product". These are the times that I wonder how somebody talked me into trying this thing.

Lets face some facts. Your an attractive woman who seems to have an interesting personality, so I imagine you get a large number of messages from random guys, of which a creepily large amount contain pictures of abs. Given this sheer volume little old me doesn't stand much of a chance of being noticed, especially since I am not gifted with the ability to start a conversation via email. I propose that, if you're in anyway interested, we cut all this crap and just get a happy hour drink sometime. At worst you lose just an hour of one day of your life.

Irregardless your above desicion. After perusing your profile I picked up a few hints that you like to run, explore Portland, and inbibe in alcoholic beverages. I guess I'm a regular Sherlock Holmes. I belong to a drinking/running group called the Hash House Harriers and I think it might be something you'd be interested in. We meet up several times a week to have a few beers, go on a run, and generally just have a good time. The two big selling points are each time it starts in a different point in the city, and only one person knows where the run is going to go.

Shawn

P.S. Kudos on looking good enough in a lavender bridesmaid dress that the dude on the motorcycle stopped to check you out.

In retrospect, women rarely like getting compared to car stereos, even highly rated ones. They say honesty is the best policy, but when it comes to online dating, that's kind of a load of bullshit.

Attempt #10: Sek8219
Sek8219's profile seemed very concerned over the possibility of a zombie apocalypse. Knowing that women like a man that makes them feel safe, I wanted to convey that I was a man of action with a plan for just such an eventuality.

I believe that everyone needs to have a zombie apocalypse escape plan. If year's of watching public service announcements has taught me anything, its be prepared.

My zombie escape plans involves an armored bus carrying at least 15 survivors with very mismatched personalities to the area of the state with the lowest population density. I envision it to be similar to MTV's Road Rules, only with zombies. I estimate that in our journey at least 5 people will die, 3 being minor characters, 1 being a major douchebag who hides the fact that he's been infected, and 1 being the most skilled character who has shown the most heroism and wisdom during the journey. When we build our new utopian city, we will name it after him/her.

Believe it or not, it worked. Probably because I was humble enough not to name the new utopian city after myself. Messages back and forth eventually led to a date, the first one I had managed to get in this mad adventure, but alas, it was not to be. Where communication via the written word had flowed like water, the spoken variety was but a trickle between us.

Attempt #11: EmRocker

Buoyed by something at least a little bit close to success, I threw myself back into the online dating world, confident that it would only be a matter of time. The next profile to catch my eye was that of EmRocker. It was a strange one, containing quite a few comments regarding slug sex. While this was obviously red flag central, my boost in confidence led me to decide that there was no risk too great. Besides, thanks to recently watching a slugcentric episode of Isabella Rosellini's *Green Porn*, a YouTube show that described how various animals mate, I had a vast knowledge of gastropod coital rituals. It almost seemed like fate.

Who isn't amazed by hot slug on slug action? Though to be honest, I have been a little traumatized since I learned that sometimes they chew each others penises off. However, regardless of my personal feelings I remember recently seeing a video on the subject and laughing my ass off. Enjoy.

Shawn

EmRocker must have already known all my slug sex fun facts and decided I had nothing new to offer because I never heard even a peep out of her.

Attempt #12: Varleigh

Varleigh's profile was one of the more enjoyable out of all the ones perused. It was a straightforward profile, succinctly not only stating who she was, but also what she wanted. It gave the impression that she had a good head on her shoulders and a realistic expectation of what a relationship entails. To add icing to the cake, her pictures gave clues that she was the kind of woman who knew how to have fun. They included one of her wearing deer horns, one of her holding a machete, and one of her holding a stack of empty beer cans taped together, better known by those in the know as a wizard's staff. How could I not message her?

Refering to what your wrote for the most private thing you're willing to admit, rock on. After reading it, and looking over the rest of your profile, a voice in my head said to me, "this woman obviously has her shit together, you should message her."

"But what the hell would I say?" I asked.

"You'll figure something out," answered the voice, "just be honest and straightforward. Also probably avoid making the obvious nice rack joke."

"C'mon, it would be hilarious." I said.

"No," said the voice forcefully, "if you want to say something about her pics complement that sweet ass machete she has, or ask her how tall she managed to get that wizard staff."

"That is a pretty rad machete."

"Indeed."

Anyway, that was the inner monologue that led to me sending this message. Maybe its a little too much for a first time message but I hope you at least get a laugh out of it. Though I would still like to know how tall that wizard staff got?

Shawn

Did it work? Damn straight it worked. I got a message back and before I knew it we had managed to have a nice long conversation centering on how tall each of us had managed to get our respective wizard staffs. Unfortunately, like all stars that shine too bright, things burned out soon after. The messages began having longer delays between them, and eventually I had to accept that things had fizzled. Such are the risks of online dating.

Attempt #13: TwoNightLights

Smarting from my latest defeat, I was glad to soon after find a profile that entertained me greatly. TwoNightLights bragged about being able to give good airplane rides, wherein one person lays on their back with their legs in the air while a second holds themselves out horizontally while balanced on the first person's feet. She also had a crazy made up story that she was going to be competing in a llama wrestling match, which apparently, at least according to her description, is more of staring contest rather than an actual grapple. Either way, it was the right combination of well thought absurdity to catch my interest.

I started writing this only hoping to score some sweet airplane rides, but then I read the rest of your profile.

Good luck to you in your upcoming Llama Wrestling competition with the unfazeable Mr. Professor. He's a dangerous opponent, and probably one of the greatest llamas to ever participate in the sport. I remember watching him during the '07 World Championship in Helsinki. He and Felipe Rostov, the reigning champ at the time, battled for over 14 hours. Finally Mr. Rostov fell over dead from a brain aneurism. For god sakes, be careful.

Shawn

P.S. Also congrats on your fine work bringing back the word heiney.

I got no response. Perhaps llama wrestling is a real thing. But then again, maybe she was just a crazy person, in which case, I'm probably better off that she never responded.

Attempt #14: BrighterQuicker

This prospective mate talked about the Urban Iditarod in her profile, an annual event where teams in coordinated costumes pull shopping carts across the city from bar to bar. Having been a participant myself in the event, it really seemed to be a no brainer. I kept it simple and did my best to try and hide the fact that I'm weird.

Realistically what kind of people haven't heard of Urban Iditarod? I've done it twice so far, once as part of the Venture Brothers team and last year as part of the probably entirely inappropriate Whitney Houston pallbearers team. What about you?

Shawn

BrighterQuicker replied. All hail the power of the Urban Iditarod. Not only did she reply, but the messages soon after led to me getting my second actual date since starting my online dating campaign. The date itself seemed to go well, with her even saying she'd be glad to have a second. But unfortunately, by the time I tried to schedule the said second date, she had apparently changed her mind. Such is life.

Attempt #15: PDXGal8

I was starting to get fed up with the whole online dating thing. Sure I had managed to get two dates, but overall it didn't seem to be worth all the work I was putting into it. Perhaps that's why things began to spiral into a strange desperation. The strategy of keeping things focused fell apart, replaced by a shotgun of openers in hopes that one would hit home. PDXGal8's profile stated that she liked poetry, wanted to go on a treasure hunt, and enjoyed talking about sociology. I went in with all guns blazing.

How do I stand out,
Just one more face in the crowd,
But so very much more.

I do not have a treasure map...yet. But I have been working on piecing together clues from old Oregon Trail journals to try and find the lost Blue Bucket Mine. This is just one of the many brands I have in the fire.

I also enjoy a talking about societal structures and theorizing on why things are the way they are. Unfortunately its often hard to find people who want to talk about such things, especially if the two of you disagree. This seems funny to me since listening to dissenting opinions is often the best way learn.

Shawn

Apparently my haiku sucked, because I never got a response.

Attempt #16: Mountain-Seeker

Things continued to degrade with each failure, though this was not how I viewed it in my mind at the time. Mountain-Seeker's profile included a lot of song lyrics, including part of a song by the Doors, so of course I thought it was clever to put in the next few lines from the song. The fact that I had to look up the lyrics online should've have been a clue that this wasn't the best of ideas. To be fair, it wasn't like her profile gave me a whole lot to work with. The only other thing of interest was that she knew how to make lemonade by letting lemons mold in water.

I see you live on Love Street
There's this store where the creatures meet
I wonder what they do in there

Lyrics from The Doors and promises to clean my fridge to make moldy lemonade. How could I resist?

My day has been a little strange. It started out normal enough with showering, shaving, eating breakfast. But then I left my wallet in the refrigerator and it has all just kind of gone downhill from there. Now here I am, wasting time, perusing the internet.

Anyways, I should probably get back to work. Message me back if you want to.

Shawn

In a word, nope. However, on the lighter side I didn't have to try lemonade made out of moldy lemons or deal with somebody who quotes song lyrics to describe themselves. So you know, silver linings.

Attempt #17: PDXrach
The experience of online dating had worn me down to a nub. With so many possibilities it was easy to find reasons to avoid messaging people, making it mean just that much more when an acceptable prospective mate presented herself. Every initial

105

message was a piece of myself. A sacrifice of time and effort to the possibility of future coupled happiness, most of which popped as easy as a soap bubble, destroying in an instant the potential world which I had created in my mind.

All together PDXrach had a pretty good profile. It was a smattering of random thoughts and factoids, a combination I would have earlier judged, but had come to accept as a mirror of my own scattered psyche. There were several parts that stuck out. In addition to a series of questions she claimed plagued her every day, she also included a joke based on the game of *Clue*, claiming that she killed a man with a pipe in the conservatory. She also bragged about her *MarioKart* abilities and had a picture of her brandishing a Christmas tree like a weapon.

Damn it, I was guessing in the billiard room with the wrench, boy was I off.

Anyways, though I am no expert and I'm absolutely not licensed in any way by any credible institution or organization, I believe I can provide suitable answers for all of the things you spend a lot of time thinking about.

You should eat food for dinner. In order to stay healthy you should avoid eating plastic fish, they are not food and present a choking hazard. The best way to get around town without a car is to learn how to fly. Learning how to fly is easy, you just throw yourself at the ground and miss. The best way to get out of town without a car is to hitchhike with truckers, they always have interesting stories and only 1 in 10 will probably murder you. For second dinner you should probably stick with food, though moss is a suitable substitute if you want to mix it up a bit. Luckily Portland has no shortage of moss, and its all organic. Thinking about your loved ones is good, though if you really cared you'd probably offer them some of your primo locally grown organic moss.

I hope this helps.

Shawn

P.S. Not to brag, but I could probably kick your ass in Mario Kart, except for Rainbow Road, that level is seriously screwed up. However, you probably have me beat in the ancient art of beating the crap out of people with Christmas trees.

Despite my best attempts it worked. I even got a pretty witty response back. Unfortunately that's where things ended. The second message was not as lucky as the first. In retrospect, it might have been for the best. Perhaps her comment regarding killing a man actually had nothing to do with *Clue*. Such is the danger of making assumptions.

With the failure of my seventeenth attempt I was completely drained. Sure I had managed to get a couple of responses and even two dates, but overall the experience was draining and decidedly strange. Not wishing to suffer the constant pain of rejection, at least for a little while, I decided to take a hiatus from the online dating world. My profile sat abandoned. Silent in the void.

My Disinheritance

My fingers move with rapid precision as they tap upon the keyboard. Letters and words magically appear before me on the monitor. I read over my creation, reach for the mouse, and hit the send key. Another email finished, another message sent into the depths of cyberspace, speeding off across miles of wires to arrive at an office only two doors down. I click back to my inbox. No new messages. My stomach gurgles, I'm hungry. It's been too long since lunch, but it's too close to quitting time to have a snack. It's time to take a break. I click through the usual websites. Facebook, Gmail, CNN, Collegehumor. Nothing new.

I adjust my slouch. My chair is too short. I am a tall man. My lower legs rest awkwardly crossed beneath my chair. My back slouches to help compensate and keep myself comfortable. My back hurts from all the damn slouching. My chair is adjustable but I can't adjust it to be high enough. My desk is too short. Instead I sit in my slouching position, slowly ruining my back and guaranteeing that I'll be slouching forever. I have asked my boss before if I could get a new desk that would actually fit me. His answer has always been a solid no. The company does not have the money. My boss is a short man, but he sits behind a very tall desk.

My gaze moves lower I and notice that my button down blue shirt has ballooned around my middle. My slouching has created extra folds of cloth that are not noticeable when I stand. The space between the bottom and second to bottom buttons has pulled apart in a way that annoys me. I run my hand around my waist, tucking my shirt deeper into my gray wool pants. It's a nervous tick, a constant battle, an unending annoyance. I was not meant to be a snazzy dresser. I'm forced to wear the clothes that I have abhorred since I was a small child. I have never liked wearing button down shirts. I have never liked tucking in my shirt. Yet here I sit, all because one must wear these clothes to be taken seriously.

My phone rings, it's someone four doors down with a question they could easily answer themselves if they weren't too lazy to open the right file on the network. The call is tedious, idle chit-chat and pleasantries. The usual about how each of us are doing, what about the big sports game, how is the weather? I cringe, wishing they would look out their own damn window. The weather isn't any different four windows down. Five minutes of this crap, followed by thirty seconds of actually answering a question. I can't blame people for wasting time. I do it myself, but for god's sake don't waste my time because you have nothing better to do.

My feet hurt. My shoes are uncomfortable. Nice shoes are always uncomfortable. By the time you have worn them long enough to make them comfortable they're too worn out to be nice shoes and you have to get new ones, and the cycle of discomfort and breaking in begins again. It's a vicious and cruel cycle. I reach down and pull up my socks. Fancy business socks in a toned down color with a simple non-offensive design on them. I abhor my socks. They wear out quickly and the elastic never seems to hold them onto my calves, especially while walking. I'm often yelled at by my boss for going barefoot around the office.

I go back to work, typing up another report that no one will ever read or pay any attention to. I am the head of the Department of Cassandric Studies. A joke. I made a sign to hang on my door until my boss made me take it down, though he didn't understand why it was funny. Cassandra, a Trojan seer who could see the future clearly, but was cursed by the gods so no one would ever believe her. I close one screen on my computer and go to open a new one, but before I do my eye catches the picture on the monitor.

The blue sky stretches all around me. The wind whispers amongst the cheat grass which grows in the thin layer of soil on the ridge tops. The valley sits below, nestled between the ridges and hills, the creek flowing through its center from the distant line of timber. Far off Mount Hood and Mount Adams dominate the skyline like ancient gods. My body sways with the horse beneath me. My hands hold the leather of the reins, smooth on one side, rough on the other. Each step rings with the sound of metal shoes against stone. The sun beats down, but my eyes are shaded by the old ball cap I wear. The day is hot, but the breeze is cooling, drying the sweat beneath my t-shirt. My nose is filled with heady smells of sage and juniper, horse sweat, and the hint of smoke from a wildfire hundreds of miles away.

Ahead of me I see six black spots standing around a tall juniper at the head of a draw. Three cows and three calves. The pace of my horse quickens. She has seen them too. The summer months are coming and it's time to move the cattle into the cool shade and long grasses of the mountains. The cows notice my approach. I can see their black heads lift and watch. They stand, chewing their cuds, patiently waiting to see what I'll do. The cows are old veterans, they've been on this same trip numerous times before. My horse gives out a loud whinny and I hear an answer off to my right. I turn and see my father riding over the crest of the hill, pushing a small herd in front of him. I pull up my horse to wait. My hands rest on the leather of my chaps.

My boss enters my office. My eyes snap off of the picture on my monitor. It's the usual bullshit. The usual crap. My boss is a paranoid man. He's constantly on the lookout for threats to his position and influence. Threats from where I do not know, but he sees them. He trusts me for some reason, and so confides his worries with me. He seems to be getting worse. He's involved in some kind of feud with another manager who is just as paranoid as he is. The two build off of each other and things are getting close to the breaking point. His latest thoughts center on an invited guest lecturer who failed to show, making my boss feel embarrassed for some reason that I don't really understand. The lecturer had called to cancel the day of, claiming a family emergency. My boss is convinced that he lied and just didn't want to show up. I don't understand, but try to assuage his fears.

My boss is older than me. He has been with the company ten years longer than I have. I can do his job better than he can. It's not something that I ever say, but I know it's true. In many ways it's my bosses paranoia that holds me back, makes it difficult to work with people in different departments. He finally leaves my office. I never knew what they meant by office politics until I actually experienced it for myself. People work their entire lives for a bullshit title and a bullshit position of leadership, and then fight tooth and nail to make sure no one else ever threatens their personal fiefdom of power. In the business world you have to watch what you say and who you say it to. You have a great idea? Too bad, the department you work for doesn't deal with that, and no one wants to hear an idea from someone they think of as an outsider. Outside ideas are meant to be feared and squashed as quickly as possible. Everyone thinks you're gunning for their job, trying to usurp them. It makes me sick.

With my boss gone the mandatory nodding of my head ceases and I try to get back to work. Reports have to be done, presentations finalized, memos sent. We are all busy as bees, productive as hell, and yet I see no difference between now and when I started three years ago. The status quo is met, you get a raise each year, maybe a fancy new title, and everybody goes home happy. I look at an email from a colleague. Another question they could easily answer themselves if they put in a little time or effort, but instead they pass the buck and send it to me. As I start to type a response the water cooler bubbles.

My pants are soaked up to my knees. They cling to my leg as I push through the tangle of the alfalfa carrying the handline. The pipe is cold in my hands. A bluebird flies past my head chirping its morning song. I smell nothing, my nose is plugged, my sinuses blocked. Twenty feet of three inch aluminum pipe. I carry it slightly off center to account for the sprinkler head which sits atop a riser on one end. Without the riser the force of the water would knock over the alfalfa. Twenty-five paces. Each pipe has to be carried twenty-five paces so it can be laid in the dry part of the field. The sun beats down on me. My feet, encased in black rubber boots, broil. A swarm of gnats fly above my head, one or two occasionally diving low enough to buzz in my ear. Twenty-five paces, thirty-two pipes, a little more water for a thirsty crop.

I step into the dry area of the field, my steps creating waves of grasshoppers that spread out before me. With a twist of my hands the pipe slides into the one before it in line. The metal clasp that holds them together clicks shut. You have to be careful. You don't want to knock out the rubber gasket that makes the seal. I stand up straight and walk back at a diagonal toward the middle of the next pipe that needs to be moved. I leave the dry dusty section of the field behind, reentering the swampy mud of the irrigated area. Zig and zag across the field. My summer morning ritual. When I finish I walk back down the line to the valve and crank it slowly so I don't kill the pump half a mile away. Water spurts from one head after another, working its way down the line. The last head begins to spin, the pipes jerk, and the sprinklers start spraying full blast. The clack of the heads drown out the sounds of the birds.

I shake myself. The shades of my youth fall back to the realities of my today. I finish the email promising that I'll get to it before the end of the week. Another project, another deadline, another movement of a cog in the belly of the great machine. An office manager comes in with something I need to sign. She is actually a secretary, but nobody calls them that anymore. At some point the word became demeaning. She chit chats for a little bit, telling me about her kids, her husband, their various weekly foibles. I politely nod and insert little quips where needed. As she talks I fidget with things on my desk, throwing away old unneeded reports and post-its. I sit glancing at my computer from time to time. I move a pen to a more strategic location. She finally runs out of steam and leaves. I check my email again. Nothing new. Again I click through a series of websites. War overseas, cute cat pictures, man nearly gets hit by car, ironic joke that isn't really ironic. Nothing really of interest, just filling time.

I would estimate that ninety percent of my work gets done in the morning. I am a morning person. I can wake up alert and get straight to work without too much screwing around. The afternoons are another story. There is something about eating lunch and then just sitting on my ass that doesn't agree with me. I become sleepy, my brain lethargic. I can't concentrate and nothing gets done. I used to worry about the amount of time I wasted during the afternoon, but my boss always compliments me on my productivity, so I guess I have no need to worry. Two co-workers stand outside my door to use the water cooler. One is telling the other about a recent camping trip.

Metal rasps against metal as I work the handle. Each movement slowly ratchets the two broken sections of barb wire closer together, tightening the fence and lifting the old wooden fence posts from the ground. My hands, encased in leather gloves, expertly tie the two ends together. The wires, now one again, are released from the spring loaded latches. The section of fence is fixed. I pick up my bucket of tools, throw the fence stretcher over my shoulder, and continue my walk along the fence line. The air is hot and humid. It seems to lay on top of me like an old woolen blanket. Tall pine and fir trees surround me, the air is heavy with their scent. Mosquitoes of all sizes buzz lazily through the thick soup that seems to weigh down everything. Few soft breezes blow through the canyon, especially this time of year. Dust motes and assorted seed pods float before me, hanging in the air as though by magic. I am alone, nobody else for miles, but I am not lonely in this wonderland.

Slowly I begin to ascend the hillside which is nothing but a slide of basalt. Rocks ranging from the size of a baseball to the size of my head. I break into the sunshine, out of the shadows, and the rocks become hot, baked on the bare slope. I can feel their heat through the rubber bottoms of my worn in leather work boots. I trudge up the hill, a machine, an automaton. My breath becomes labored, but I do not take any rests until I reach the top. My mouth hangs open, letting air bypass my stuffy nose. I count myself lucky. I only have to walk along the fence as it climbs up the hill. I didn't have to build the god awful thing. It's probably over fifty years old. The slight wind is hot, like stirring soup fresh from the stove. The trees wave below me and Indian Paintbrush daubs the hill with bright flashes of orange in several shades. When I get to the top I can go home, the day's work accomplished.

My face explodes in a sneeze, blowing away the memories. I shake my head and look at the clock on my monitor. It's nearly five o'clock, nearly time to go home. Daydreams, nothing more than daydreams. The thoughts of an unoccupied mind. It's so easy to remember all of the good things, to forget the bad. When you're not actually suffering from them, it's so easy to forget how bad the problems were. The subconscious memories are always the romantic version. It's the conscious part of your mind that remembers why things are the way they are. It's the conscious part that remembers the bone dry and swollen sinuses, the constant sneezing, the runny red rimmed eyes half swollen shut, the constant throb of headaches that turned into sharp knives when I bent over. The doctors give it all sorts of names and explanations, but in the end they always say there is nothing they can do. My body betrayed me.

It's five o'clock. I power down my computer, pick up my briefcase and push my chair back under my desk. I flick out the lights as I walk out the door. This is not the life that I would have chosen for myself. These are not the things that I once dreamed about. But this is what I have. I work hard. I am successful. I am respected. I am an exile.

Addiction

Some people are like heroin. Every time you're around them you feel happy, giddy, on top of the world. It's an amazing feeling. It's a rare thing to find somebody who can make you feel that way. Somebody who can help you feel more and see more than you ever have before. These in themselves are not bad things. These aren't things to be avoided, but rather embraced. But sometimes the consequences are too high. Sometimes the long term bad outweighs the short term good.

Some people draw you in, pull you toward them until you're nothing but a moon orbiting their gravitational field. Sometimes they're bad people. Sometimes they're good people who have their own problems, which makes them do bad things. It's always there. No matter how much you enjoy yourself, no matter how much you laugh and smile when you're around them. Beneath all the comfort and elation is a quiet voice in the back of your mind, trying to warn you that this is a bad idea. We as humans crave happiness, comfort, a feeling of acceptance. We need these things, we are addicted to them. We look for them with a desperation that borders on insanity.

Sometimes we find a source that gives us everything we think we need, but slowly drains the life from us. For every high we slowly fall deeper in, until we can't imagine feeling that high with anyone else. We trap ourselves in bad situations. We erode our own confidence and self-esteem. We become dependent, addicted. Who's to blame in such a situation? The heroin hurts us, but we are the ones who choose to partake. It's hard to quit. It's hard to forget. It's hard to come down off of that high.

Withdrawal is full of pain and yearning, fear and confusion. The poison calls out to us like a siren, an instant cure for what ails us. It will be okay. Things will be different this time. There is nothing to be afraid of. Come back and feel the bliss. Lies. It doesn't matter if they come from someone else's mouth or our own. To me, some people are like heroin, and nobody worth a shit wants anything to do with a heroin addict.

How I Was Almost Deaf

I don't know if it's still this way, but when I was a kid all the students in a certain age group were required to take a hearing and eye test at school. At some point the government had discovered that not being able to see or hear may act as a major detriment to a student's ability to learn. Thanks to this amazing piece of insight, every year from kindergarten through fourth grade we walked one by one out of our classroom to make sure what were deemed our most important senses were working correctly.

Eye and hearing test day was always a good day in school. It was considered wrong for a teacher to continue trying to shove our brains full of information when at least one student was constantly gone. So instead, we got to enjoy a myriad of activities. If you had a fun teacher you got to read books, play games, or do puzzles. If you had a teacher who actually cared about your education, you got math problems and book reports. Though I was not appreciative at the time, most of my teachers were of the latter category.

Sitting around doing math problems is never fun for a child of eight. You sit there furiously working out what the remainder is if 97 is divided by 6, watching with half an eye as another lucky kid gets to throw down their pencil and take the long walk across the school to the art room. There seemed to be no rhyme or reason to how the students were called up. They were not in alphabetical order, last name or first, order by birthday, or even order by height. For all I knew they could have been drawing a name out of a hat, except every kid knows hats are not allowed in school.

As each kid finished their test they were given the next random name to take back to their classroom, a small little taste of power in a world where we had none. They would walk in, their chests puffed out, secure in their knowledge that they were enjoying the auditory and visual world at peak optimal efficiency. With a high pitched bellow they would call out the next name, only to crash them back to Earth as the teacher shushed them and set them back to doing math problems. Their short time of power gone, they would slump back in their desks and watch with jealousy as the next kid rose and headed out the door.

I've never been good at waiting. As the clock ticked, my pencil would begin tapping the desk in time. As each name was called my body would jerk with momentary and involuntary excitement until I realized that it was not my name. I'd then fall back in disappointment, pent up energy bursting out in tiny fidgets. Tick-tock, tick-tock goes the clock. Tap, tap, tap, tap goes my pencil. Ding, ding, ding, ding goes my foot against the desk leg. Cluck, cluck, cluck goes my tongue.

"Shawn, stop that and get back to work on your math problems."

My teacher's voice cuts through the silence, and the numerous little faces with which I share my tiny world snap up to look at me in amusement, glad to see someone besides them get corrected. I quickly settle my body, face red with embarrassment, and try to concentrate on my mathematics. The sound of the door opening pierces the silence, a squeaky hinge like an exclamation point. I tense, but I refuse to look, refuse to let my excitement get the better of me again. The shrill voice of my classmate, a tone of authority, pierces the room.

"Shawn Campbell."

My body leaps out of my desk, my pencil goes flying, my classmate has become my rescuer. I land loudly, both feet hitting the floor at the same time. My teacher gives me a stern look. I pick up my pencil and walk demurely out the door. As soon as I'm in the hallway I throw my shoulders back and strut, going at a speed that will guarantee the maximum amount of time to reach my destination without anyone asking where the hell I've been. The art room, where the tests are administered, is clear across the school in the wing that holds the junior high students.

It's a little like going to Neverland. The walls are all covered in lockers, big metal boxes holding the secrets of a future world. Strange smells emit from the bathrooms where the toilets sit up higher than the ones on my end of the school. The big kids mill about between classes, talking in strange tongues, using mysterious code words like algebra, Shakespeare, and French kissing. I shrink down to the size of a mouse as I pass through this strange world of giants, not wanting to be seen. I arrive at my destination and raise my tiny hand to tap at the door. The special ed teacher opens it and welcomes me into her lair.

The room has always been called the art room, but the only thing I ever really remember doing in it is taking eye and hearing tests. Brushes, paint, old dried clay, and a paper mache donkey all give clues to its former glory. Now it's only a little shadowy room filled with dust and the shattered dreams of countless students who discovered they did not have the talent to transfer the creations of their minds into a physical form. I cough and shift quietly as the special ed teacher explains how everything is going to work. I don't listen. This is my third time taking the test. I'm an old hand. Instead I watch dust motes float in the light of the window.

First comes the vision test. She hands me a large plastic spoon to hold in front of each eye as I recite letters off an old yellowed poster hung on the wall. First the left eye and then the right. Read off each line. Go down as far as you can. I always squint a bit as I get down to the smaller rows, the tiny letters becoming indistinct and blurred. The special ed teacher marks notes on a piece of paper, says good, and then tells me to switch to the other eye. The right eye is always easier. I do not have to squint as hard because I have already memorized all the letters from when I was using my left eye. More notes and more statements of a job well done. I'm asked to sit to start the hearing test.

The hearing test consists of a big blocky machine from the 1960s and a giant pair of oversized headphones that completely encase my ears. As she flips on the machine the special ed teacher smiles and gives me directions.

"All right Shawn, you're going to hear a tone in either your left ear, your right ear, or both ears. When you hear the beep I want you to raise your hand on the side you hear it on. Do you understand?"

I nod my head.

"Okay, let's get started."

She fiddles with the machine, presses a button, and looks at me expectantly. I sit and stare blankly back at her. Her face scrunches up and she fiddles with the machine more, presses another button, and looks at me again. Not knowing what else to do I smile at her, waiting for the test to get started.

"Shawn, did you hear anything?"

"No."

Her face scrunches more, lines of worry spreading from her forehead. More fiddling with knobs, her hands moving quickly, but less sure. She hits the button again.

"How about now?"

"No."

Now I start to become worried. My eight year old brain is catching up with the situation. I'm supposed to hear something, but I'm not. This is probably not good. I watch in abject horror as she continues to twist knobs and hit buttons, staring at me, willing me to give some kind of reaction.

The special ed teacher stops messing with the hearing test machine and peers at me. She speaks in a slow measured voice, her mouth over emphasizing every movement of her lips and tongue.

"Shaaawwnnn....... Caaannn...yooouuu...heeaaarrr...meee?"

My reply matches the slow pace of the question, drawing out the single word.

"Yeeessss."

The special ed teacher looks puzzled. She begins flipping the machine on and off. Its steady hum falls and rises. She plays with the knobs and buttons again, stops, looks at me, and goes back to frantically messing with the machine. She gets out of her seat and goes to the plug in the wall, pulls it out and puts it back in. I become bored. My eyes begin to wander across the room, taking in the all the knick knacks and left behind creations of imagination scattered across the shelves and counters along the walls. My hands begin to play with the wire of the headphones, twirling it in my fingers. Slowly I pull up the slack of the long cord into a pile on my lap, wishing I could go back to my classroom.

My fingers work without me watching them. My eyes follow the frantic special ed teacher. The soft rubber turns to cold metal in my hand. I look down. I'm holding the headphone jack in my hand. I stare at it for a few seconds, and then realization dawns like a sunrise across my mind. Whoever had gone before me had unplugged the headphones when they had taken them off. The special ed teacher turns around and sees the jack in my hand. Her scrunched up worried face melts into relief. Silently she takes the headphone jack, plugs it into the hearing test machine, and turns it back on. The gentle hiss of white noise fills my ears. The special ed teacher smiles with triumph as she pushes the button.

BEEP!!!

I jump nearly out of my seat in horror and surprise as the noise batters its way into my ear and ricochets through my skull. The special ed teacher jumps as well, the look of worry momentarily returning. She then smiles, reaches down, and confidently twists the knob that lowers the volume.

Blow Job

I look down at her and her efforts. I know they are futile but I'm not yet willing to admit that to her, because to do so would be to admit it to myself. I lay weak and limp, her head in my lap giving her all for the sole goal of giving me pleasure, but I do not care. I can't get myself to care. I feel dead inside. I know it must be strange for her. To be doing everything she can and getting little to no reaction in return. I want to speak up, to tell her that it's not her fault. That the problem has nothing to do with her. I want to tell her everything. I want to tell anybody everything, but I hold my tongue, and hide in my own head.

She's a physically attractive woman, tight body and dark Mediterranean skin. She's a good person. You get the sense that she tries to do the right thing. She's a friend of a friend. A blind date set up and carried forward into further self-planned dates. I find conversation with her boring. She likes to talk about nice things, normal things, sweet things. I found the first conversation with her boring, the latest conversation with her boring, and all the conversations in between boring. Yet here I am.

It's a sick thing to say. A fucked up thing to say. This woman is not a person to me. She is a thing. She is only a distraction. I know that there's no future in what I'm doing. I know that this will never lead to anything. I'm a prisoner in my own mind. I yearn to be free, but I can't get out. Being with her is akin to throwing a baseball against the wall in my mental cell. There are so many other things that I wish I was doing, but without their possibility this is better than nothing. The alternative of being alone and stuck with myself seems more frightening than my own moral decay.

Why? Why did it all happen? Was there something I missed? Was there something that I could have done? I can't keep my mind on the moment. It keeps traveling back to the place that I'd rather be. The person I'd rather be with. The feelings I have are frightening. I don't know how to control them. I wish they would go away and leave me at peace. This woman is a poor distraction, but it's not her fault.

It's all fucked up. I know what I'm doing is wrong. Many people will point out that the world is not black and white, that everything is mostly gray. They would point out that this woman is responsible for herself and how she reacts to the situations she finds herself in. I try to believe it, but in my mind it's all horse shit. If you know that you're going to hurt somebody needlessly, and do it anyway, you are doing the wrong thing. The world of gray is a creation for those who have done wrong and can't face it or admit to it. An illusion hiding the fact that if the same thing was done to them they would be pissed off. I'm taking advantage of someone else's loneliness, someone else's need to feel a connection, and it's wrong.

I lay with her head in my lap and think of other women. I think of being other places. This is not where I want to be. I don't like to be treated the way I am treating this woman. I don't like being treated like a thing instead of a person of equal complexity and depth. Guilt. That's the root of the problem. That's the root of my difficulty. I'm not ready to be with someone else. I should not be with her. Even if I was fine I doubt I would want to be with her. The entire thing is a lie, a comforting daydream brought to life, but I cannot escape fully from reality. Her eyes look up into mine.

"Is anything happening?"

I look down at her and fake a smile.

"I must have had too many beers tonight. Lets just go to sleep."

"All right."

She scoots up the bed and lays her head on my shoulder. She breathes in deep and exhales. I hope she believes my lie. I hope she doesn't think that it's some shortcoming of hers. There's a part of me that still cares about the people around me. Part that swears to do no harm. However, there's another selfish part. A selfish and scared part that hopes she doesn't realize exactly how fucked up I am.

I am all fucked up. My mind has become a prison. I look back and imagine the happier world that I once inhabited. Where things seemed so much more light and carefree. The world I imagine is an illusion, but yet I miss it. The only difference between then and now is the fact that I risked becoming attached enough to feel the difference when it was gone. I'm trying to plug leaks with anything I can find, but at the same time hide the fact that my boat is sinking.

I need to break up with this woman. I need to set her free. Let her go. It's the right thing to do. I'm being selfish and not doing the right thing. It's obvious to me, but yet I can't get myself to do it. There's a part of me that hopes that if I hold on a little longer, maybe I can get myself to say the things that are all buried inside. To trust someone enough to talk about it again. Like a house closed up all winter, I need to open the windows, for everything has grown stale and started to stink. I yearn for the ability to talk about all that has happened. I yearn for it just as deeply as I yearn for all that I have lost.

The hope is a false one. I know that I will never tell her all the things that are making me such a shitty person. The things that fill me with guilt and despair. I fear rejection. I want to be the one who rejects, not the one who is rejected. It's ridiculous. How can someone fear rejection from something they don't even want? I'm living in a paradox of my own selfish needs. I want her out of my life, but I want to be the one who makes the decision.

I feel her breathing begin to become more rhythmic and regular. She has fallen asleep. I carefully pull my arm out from under her head. I lay awake, separate from her, staring upward at the ceiling, wishing for someone to comfort me. I begin to tremble. I hope she doesn't feel it through the mattress. My mind tracks back over the past year and tries to make sense of what makes no sense. Every word and every action is permanently etched into my brain. I watch it all like a movie. Why? Why did she do the things she did? Why couldn't she tell me what was wrong? It's so much easier to remember the problems of the past then to solve the ones of the present. My mouth opens and my words spill out into the darkness, onto ears that cannot hear.

The Purpose Of Life

People once struggled to understand the difference between our physical and mental selves. While the functions of our bodies could be studied and tested, our amazing minds remained a mystery. Philosophers and mystics once thought of everyone as being made up of two parts. The body, the physical, a container of matter in different states. The mind, our soul, an ethereal spirit, a ghost whose abilities would be boundless if it was not trapped in the fragile body. In today's modern world we know better, though many don't like to admit it. The body is not a vehicle for our soul. Rather the body is its creator.

All of our thoughts, dreams, hopes, fears, and emotions are just controlled bursts of electrical energy and chemical reactions.

When we learn our body creates new cells and new connections between cells. When we feel fear our body releases a domestically manufactured hormone which elicits a pre-programmed response. When we feel attachment a different hormone is released, eliciting the pre-programmed response we call love. We are but a machine, an amazing machine albeit, but still just a machine. We are built and programmed by our environment and time. All of life is a machine, but only the human race is broken. Of all the machines in the natural world, we are the only ones that are self-aware enough to guarantee our own demise.

We question. No other species questions itself like we do. No other species feels the need to find the logic behind its actions, to question why it does things, or to question whether to some outside viewer those actions could be seen as right or wrong. It is this ability to question all that we do that makes us human. It is a strange trait for a life form to develop, the ability to question, the ability to feel that something is not right.

We are inefficient. Every other life form has developed to be as efficient as possible in the world that they find themselves in. We are the only species that has changed ourselves, not because the environment has changed around us, but because the development of our brains has changed how we perceive the world. We have created a world within our heads. A mental world that shapes our evolutionary tract just as much as the physical world around us.

We question and make complex what is simple. The purpose of life is simple. It is to propagate and ensure the survival of the future members of our species. To guarantee that we survive long enough to meet this goal, we all have to meet our basic needs of food, water, and shelter. All of our science and civilization is based off the need to consistently alleviate these basic needs to give our offspring the best chance. All of it is just our unique adaptation to survive the world around us. We have gotten so good at meeting our basic needs that we no longer need the powerful brains we developed to figure out how best to meet them.

All of the rest - art, entertainment, curiosity, philosophy - was created just because our brains have gotten bored. Our bodies have allergic reactions because we are too clean and our immune systems don't have enough to do. All of our culture is just an allergic reaction. We are allowed to put value on things that have no value in the ultimate purpose of life, because the basic needs that we require are so easy to obtain. From this evolution comes all of our needs for spiritual fulfillment and complex emotions. These complex needs are of the utmost importance to us, until the basic needs that sustain them are no longer present. When our basic needs go unsated, the world that we have built for ourselves within ourselves collapses like a house of cards, blown over by a single puff of real wind.

This is all either brilliant, or complete bullshit.

The Colonel

"I'm sorry I'm late, I had to give my cat his medicine."

"Your cat?"

"Yes, my cat, Colonel Flufferbottoms."

"Colonel Flufferbottoms?"

"Yes, my cat, Colonel Flufferbottoms."

"You have a cat named Colonel Flufferbottoms?"

"Yes."

"Since when?"

"Since I was a child. Christ, it's like you don't even know me."

"Sorry. It's just……"

"It's just what?"

"It just seems like a bit of a ridiculous name for a cat. That's all."

"Not really. Cats are very dignified animals. Almost too dignified if you ask me. That's why I always give them names that look very dignified, but when you say them out loud they sound ridiculous. You know, so you keep them knocked down a notch without wounding their pride. The Colonel is an especially dignified cat, so I think his name fits him quite well."

"Dignified? Your cat?"

"Oh yeah, he's by far the most dignified cat I've ever owned. He always acts very proper, a regular fur covered little gentleman. None of that pouncing and playing that you see other cats do, nope, not Colonel Flufferbottoms. He always sits at rapt attention and watches with a steady appraising gaze."

"Appraising?"

"Yeah, appraising, you know, evaluating, assessing. Mind you, it's not a judgmental gaze, but it definitely reminds you that you could do better."

"The cat tells you that you could do better?"

"Not directly, but he definitely makes you think about your life.

"What?"

"It's not what you think."

"But...."

"I've never known a better cat. When we sit and talk in the evening he always proves to be the most understanding and steady friend that I've ever had."

"When you talk? To your cat?"

"Yeah, when we talk. The Colonel and I often wile away the evening hours discussing life, love, the world, and needed socio-economic reforms. He's an old cat, near twenty three years, and you can tell that his opinions are derived from a great deal of experience and deep thought."

"His opinions?"

"Are, like I said, obviously well thought out. Hell, just the other day the Colonel was deep into his fifth saucer of brandy and....."

"Wait, your cat drinks brandy?"

"Of course. The Colonel and I like to enjoy a nightcap together every evening. He usually has about three to four saucers full. I only have one, you know, because one of us has to get up for work in the morning."

"You drink brandy with your cat? Out of a saucer?"

"God no, don't be ridiculous. I drink mine out of a snifter."

"Brandy....Your cat....."

"Yep, every evening."

"Why brandy?"

"The Colonel believes that brandy is the only true choice for a gentleman's nightcap. He says, and mind you I'm only quoting here, that you never saw a god damn Mick passed out in the street from drinking too much brandy."

"A god damn Mick?"

"Yes, an Irishman. I fear I must apologize for the Colonel. Though he is a fairly fine fellow, he can be a little racist at times against certain ethnicities. For instance, he especially hates the Siamese."

"The Siamese? You mean people from Southeast Asia?"

"No, I mean Siamese cats."

"Siamese cats?"

"Yes, he absolutely cannot stand to be in the presence of Siamese cats. Flies into a hissing rage every time he comes near one. I wish that he would change, but it's difficult to change the opinions of a twenty three year old cat, and I've long given up on trying."

"But...."

"Anyway, as I was saying. The Colonel was telling me about his ancestor Gustav."

"Gustav?"

"Yes, Gustav. The Colonel often tells me about his family when he's deep into his saucers. He's very proud of them. He loves to talk about his ancestor Ludwig, who was the personal cat of General Erwin Rommel. Ludwig joined the General on his campaigns across North Africa."

"I never knew the Desert Fox had a cat."

Oh yes, Ludwig was with the General through everything, right up until the General's heroic suicide to save his family."

"Nasty business that."

"Quite. Anyway, I was talking about Gustav. Gustav rarely comes up in our conversations. The Colonel likes to claim that his ancestors were the Royal Mousers for the Kaisers in Berlin, but that's not the truth."

"No."

"Yes. He told me the truth one night when the saucers made his head and tongue light. The Von Flufferbottoms can actually only trace their lineage back to a stray named Gustav who lived in the German trenches during the First World War."

"No."

"Yes. He told me how Gustav used to comfort the soldiers when things would get their worst. He lived in the trenches with them, surviving on rats, random scraps, and his own fallen comrades in arms."

"What?"

"He partook nourishment from the bodies of fallen soldiers."

"That's horrible."

"That's what I said, but the Colonel, the Colonel looked me straight in the eye and told me I should not judge Gustav, for I have never lived the life of a cat in a First World War trench."

"But still...."

"No, he told me, you cannot judge. Gustav only did what was most natural to us all, he survived."

"I guess. It's all just pretty disturbing when you think about it. But wait, if his family lived in Germany, how did the Colonel get to America."

"That's another story that the Colonel only told me when he was deep in his saucers. Apparently his great grandfather was owned by a German prostitute who fell in love with an American GI at the height of the Cold War. They married and she moved with him back to the States, taking only the few things she owned. A large walnut dresser, a bag full of skimpy negligee, and the Colonel's great grandfather."

"It sounds like the Colonel has a lot of skeletons in his closet."

"Indeed he does, but as the Colonel says, aside from death, family is the only thing about ourselves we cannot change. I wouldn't say that the Colonel is ashamed of his family's past mind you, he just doesn't like to bring it up in front of others. I made the mistake once of trying to joke with him about it. He spent the next week shitting in the kitchen cupboard and clawing me during his daily belly rub."

"What?"

"Yes, yes, I know what you're thinking. Belly rubs are not that dignified."

"Actually I....."

"But as the Colonel says, even the noblest of the noble deserve to have one little pleasure in life. Even if it's so ridiculous that one must hide it from his contemporaries."

"That actually sounds like pretty good advice. He sounds like one hell of a cat."

"Indeed. Indeed he is. It's just too bad he probably won't be with us much longer."

"Is he sick?"

"Yeah, that's why he takes medication."

"Is it bad?"

"Quite, I'm afraid the Colonel has diabetes."

"That's terrible."

"It is. The worst of it is that he must be given his medicine three times a day."

"That sounds....."

"And the medicine is a suppository."

"Shit."

"Yep. But you should see him. I don't believe anyone else in the world could manage to still look so dignified while getting a large pill shoved up his ass. He always waits patiently and never curses or acts in any way impolite, even when my hands are cold."

"How noble of him."

"Indeed, but that's not the worst of his troubles."

"No?"

"No. Despite his medicine I'm afraid the diabetes advanced too far. They had to amputate his right front foot a few months back."

"That sucks."

"It sucked big time. But I'm afraid that was just the beginning of his troubles."

"Why? What happened?"

"When he went in for the surgery the doctor misread his chart, and instead of cutting off just his front right foot, the doctor cut off his entire front right leg."

"Oh my god."

"That's what the Colonel said when he came to after the surgery and found out. Even then he was dignified. When he looked down at where his leg used to be he asked calmly for everyone but the doctor to leave the room. The Colonel tried to hide it, but you could tell that he was furious. I don't know what the Colonel said to that doctor, but when the doctor came out he was white as a sheet and covered in scratches. I don't think I've ever seen the Colonel have such an outburst before."

"You can hardly blame the Colonel for that."

"Heavens no, of course not. If I was in his place I doubt I could have restrained myself like he did. That doctor cost the Colonel his leg and got off lightly in my mind. I wanted to write a letter to the American Association of Veterinary State Boards and have his license revoked. But the Colonel would have none of that. He said that mistakes happen and that it's pointless to dwell on the past."

"He's certainly a better person than I would be in that situation."

"Me too. The Colonel though, he even gave the doctor a dead bird, you know, just to show there were no hard feelings."

"Still though, what a tragedy."

"Not to the Colonel, he didn't even let it slow him down. He refused to get a prosthetic, said he didn't want to depend on anything he didn't come into this world with. Instead, he put in a lot of time and effort, and eventually got himself to the point where he could get around better on three legs than most cats can get around on four."

"Good for him. That's pretty inspiring, you know, for a cat."

"Yeah, it's just too bad that lately he's been slowly taking a turn for the worst. I know he's an old cat, but still, it's hard to watch him go downhill."

"I'm sorry to hear it."

"It just breaks my heart to seem him still try to put forward an air of dignity and grace, even as he's forced to spend most of his days in bed, losing control of his bowels. It's....it's just so damn hard."

"I'm so very sorry."

"It's okay. I'm just going to miss him, that's all. Once he goes that will be the end of the Von Fluffenbutter family line."

"He never had any kittens?"

"Oh, I'm sure there are quite a few. The Colonel was fairly wild in his younger days. But he never got married, and the Colonel absolutely refuses to recognize a bastard as one of his own. It's his damn pride. It's....it's....it's just too bad. I'm sure they would be a comfort to him now. But you just can't change a twenty three year old cat. It's just how things are. Anyway, sorry again I was late."

"Don't give it a second thought okay. Let me buy you a drink."

"Buy me a drink? Really?"

"Yeah, we can get a drink and then make a toast to your amazing cat."

"Thanks, that would be great. A toast. A toast to Colonel Von Fluffynutter."

"Yeah.....wait. Did you just call him Colonel Von Fluffynutter?"

"Yeah, what else would I call him."

"You told me his name was Colonel Von Flufferbottoms."

"What?"

"You said his name was Colonel Von Flufferbottoms."

"Ummmm...."

"What the hell? Was all of that just bullshit?"

"......."

"Seriously, what the hell?"

"Okay, okay, I made the whole thing up. Colonel Von Fluffer...whatever doesn't exist."

"What the fuck, did you seriously just talk with me for half an hour about an imaginary cat? That's really fucked up. Are you insane?"

"I don't think so. I feel pretty sane."

"So then why the hell were you late?"

"I....."

"Well?"

"I missed the bus."

"Why the hell did you miss the bus?"

"I don't want to say."

"You wasted my time with this crap and now you can't even tell me the truth?"

"I……"

"Why did you miss the god damn bus?"

"Because I was taking a pee behind a dumpster in an alley."

"What?"

"I really had to pee."

"Unbelievable. I don't have time for your shit today. I'm leaving."

"Wait. What if the Colonel is real and we're the ones that are imaginary?"

"Goodbye."

"Bye."

Golden Tears

My foot slipped from the rock where it was precariously perched and fell into the creek. My socks and boots were quickly soaked through. Seeing no reason to continue my hop-skip routine I simply walked the rest of the way across the creek, cussing as I went. There was no reason not to cuss, I was all alone on a dirt road about a mile from my house. Only the stunted trees along the hay field could hear me and they never bothered to berate me for my choice of language.

The coldness of my feet only added to the bleakness of the day. I don't know what caused the bleakness. Maybe it was because of the mind-numbing chores I had done all day, the kind that require repetitive movement with little or no thinking involved. Maybe it was just how the weather was in general. It was a cold autumn day where the clouds blocked the sky and made everything dark and gray. One of those days where you can taste the crispness of the air and feel an energy all around from winter closing in. No birds sang and nothing moved. Not even the wind rustled the tree branches.

I continued my desolate walk up the dirt road toward home, my feet stirring no dust as I plodded down that trodden path. On either side of me trees stripped by the season of their greenness stood like skeletal sentries. All was quiet and colorless in the world this autumn day had thrown me into. Only the clouds above me moved on their lonely march across the endless skies, waiting to release winter's first snow and send our world into hibernation.

Usually I wouldn't have noticed it, but my senses were so dulled that any color seemed bright and vibrant. It stopped me short when I saw it, a single leaf, dull colored, shaded the same as dried blood. If it had been on any other day I wouldn't have noticed it, but in the grayness the leaf seemed to shine like vibrant gold. Like the way food tastes sweeter to a starved man, the leaf seemed so colorful, thanks to my own deprivation. As I watched it the leaf finally gave up its death grip on the tree and fell to Earth, floating on a bed of air, touching the ground without a sound.

I alone saw the leaf fall, and for some reason, as it did, it started me thinking. We're all just like the leaf, doomed from the beginning to someday have to let go, knowing that when we do, it's possible that no one will notice our passing. No tear came to my eye as I thought of this, no sadness filled my soul, for I continued to think of the leaf.

Like us it had been born into a world that was fresh and new. Gentle rains caressed it like a mother's loving hands, all was good and healthy in the world. As its life continued into the golden days of summer, it slowly got older. Its edges dried and curled, bugs and other pests chewed pieces from it. Time started to wear away at it, just like a person who starts to feel the pains of age. Then comes the autumn and the last of the greenness of its youth disappears from its skin. Its age is apparent to all. It holds on as long as it can, but like all things, it can't escape its final fate.

To some this may seem like the foretelling of the doom that awaits us all, but this is not how I felt on that day. That one falling dead leaf was possibly the most beautiful sight I've ever seen. No wind brushed it loose. It fell like it knew that its time had come. The leaf floated in the air for the longest time, softly, like it was cupped in angel hands, hands that tenderly fondled it and spoke soft words to it, telling it everything would be all right. When the leaf hit the ground it left no impression, but instead seemed to caress the cold earth like an old friend.

All of these thoughts passed through my mind just as the leaf fell to the ground. By the time it finally hit the Earth, I had realized that death was not a thing to be feared, but to be welcomed. For like the life that it ends, it is beautiful, and after the coldness of winter, spring will always come again. Death is not punishment, but a reward of rest for a life that was lived as well as possible.

I started to walk, no longer noticing my surroundings, my head filled with deep thoughts. My shadow crossed the leaf like a death pall. I looked down on it and stared for a full minute. I can't tell you what went through my head, for it was such a storm of confusion that nothing came through clearly. I slowly bent over and picked it up, cupping it protectively in my hand. As I looked at that crinkled brown piece of matter a tear filled my eye. It flowed down my cheek and fell to the ground, a solitary tear for a solitary leaf. Sadness filled my soul, but yet that dead leaf still seemed so beautiful. I carried it home, in many ways still not knowing why.

Characters

For each of us, the theater of our lives contains three different kinds of characters. Primary characters, secondary characters, and extras. The vast majority of people are just extras. People in the background. People we don't notice. They are the people we walk past on the street. The people we wait in line with at the grocery store. The people driving the other cars that wait with us at traffic lights. They have little to no effect on our lives and in our minds they are just part of the landscape.

Occasionally we come to the realization that this sea of faces represents other people. People just as complex and amazing as ourselves. People with dreams, worries, fears, joys, and hidden secrets. For a moment, looking at the sea of anonymous faces is comparable to looking up at the stars. All that you are shrinks down until you are small and insignificant. The world becomes overwhelmingly big and we are forced to turn the faces back into anonymous objects to keep our sanity.

Secondary characters are people that are a regular part of our lives. They do the same activities, work at the same office, eat at the same deli, and hang out with the same group of people. However, they have no significant impact on our lives. We talk with them from time to time, but never about anything important. They are acquaintances, not friends. We are aware of their lives, with all their ups, downs, and random bullshit, but we don't care. Watching their lives unfold is like watching a television show. We watch the drama, but can walk away at any moment without a second thought.

Primary characters are the people in our lives who have an impact. We have an impact on them, they have an impact on us. They play a major part in the plotline of our lives. They are our parents, our close friends, our siblings, our mentor, our nemesis. They are the people we care about. The ones that bring out the best and the worst in us. We are interested in what these people have to say. We notice these people when they walk into a room. We notice when they are gone.

Home Sweet Home

My wrist clenches tighter and the screw driver twists, pushing the screw deeper into the wood I hold against the door frame. Force and torque, tools and energy, that is all it takes to attach the rough cut pine board to the back door of my house. The edge of the board is broken. Two straight lines created by a hacksaw that never meet in the middle, connected by a jagged break. A hacksaw is not made for sawing boards, but it's what I have, so I make it work. The jagged middle is a sign of my impatient nature. The sawing of the board with the hacksaw is slow compared to the quick downward thrust of a leg. I smile as the screw spins deeper. A homeowner's work is never done.

My house is a nice house. It has a nice bedroom. The bedroom is the largest that I've ever had. The wasted space is a luxury. My bed is awash in a sea of hardwood. My bedroom has a large closet which does not have doors. Inside are my clothes, hanging in rows and sitting in my dresser. My clothes are not alone inside the dresser. Inside the top drawer are also six Durex condoms, Trojans always seem to break, and a sock stuffed with a huge roll consisting of one-hundred-and-twenty-nine one dollar bills. My wallet always inexplicably fills with one dollar bills to the point where it can barely close. The sock seemed like a good solution. Plus it feels pretty badass to have a huge roll of money, even if it's only small denominations.

The board is attached and I move back to admire my handy work in the dim light of the garage. The board sits squarely on top of its twin across the top of the door's window, blocking the inrush of cold night air from outside. Each of the two boards is held on by four screws. Each screwed in by hand. My electric drill no longer works, its battery is aged long past its expected lifespan. The boards block the night air, but they also block the entry of the outside light, which illuminates the patio. Not perfect, but it will work for now. Only a temporary scar on my house.

My house has a nice second bedroom, but I use it for an office. The office is slightly smaller than my bedroom, but still comfortably sized. It also has a large closet, though this one is just full of random junk. Things that need a space, but have no specific place to go. A small futon loveseat sits in one corner. Two bookcases cover one wall. The left one overrun with classics, renowned authors, and books of thought and depth. The right one is filled with Star Wars books, a monument to a youthful obsession. A desk sits in one corner. On top of it is my new PC computer, an impulse buy, an amazing step forward in our world of technology. Inside the top drawer is my laptop. In the lower drawer are my taxes, credit card statements, passport, and social security card. All of the documentation that proves that I actually exist.

I open the door and the cold darkness rushes into the garage. I shiver involuntarily. A pane of glass sits outside on the patio, delicately placed, a large piece broken off one corner. It should be replaced, but it is all I have tonight. Clear packaging tape provides the answer to the question of how to fix the problem. It has the combined attributes of both working and being available. Plenty is still lying around from the move several months ago. It's a simple fix. Put the two pieces of glass together and tape. Is it enough? Probably, but I put another two pieces of tape across the whole pane in an X anyways. It doesn't hurt, and it will at least hold everything together if the glass breaks again.

My house has a nice living room. Four floor to ceiling windows wrap a corner, letting in the light each morning. Before moving into my house I used to never own much furniture, but the little bit that I had seemed so alone that I felt the need to purchase it more companions. Two chairs, a couch, and a coffee table. It almost looks like the home of some kind of responsible adult. Two lamps light the room, one tall one in the corner, and one small green one sitting on an end table next to the easy chair that I rarely sit in. The easy chair was once my uncle's, but he has made a journey and now it is mine. A fireplace sits in the center of one wall, its mantle covered by knick-knacks from my travels. A television and gaming console sit on a stand in one corner. Two closets open onto the living room. One holds games, camping supplies, and other random things. The second holds coats, a vacuum cleaner, and a twenty-two caliber rifle.

I hold the glass up to its place on the door frame with one hand, pushing it up and under the top and left side edging. My other hand picks up and holds the lower edging in place, trapping the window, making it part of the door. The lower and right side edging have been ripped aside. Large pieces of paint from the door hang from their sides. The small nails that once held the lower edging in place slide back into the holes from which they had been wrenched. The paint lines up perfectly with the areas of door once bare. It's no longer enough to hold it in place. My hammer and three penny nails quickly solve the problem. I reach down and pick up the right side window edging. My belly grumbles. I'm hungry, it is late, already past midnight, and I have not yet had a chance to eat.

My house has a nice dining room. It is small, with only a round table surrounded by four chairs. I am quite proud of the table. You can unlatch a few clasps and pull it apart, turning the circle into a large oval. The extension piece is part of the table, it simply folds out into place, attached by hinges which hide it underneath when not in use. In one corner on a stand sit two ends of the auditory technology timeline. An old record player, another impulse buy, with only two records sitting below it. An old portable unit like the ones I remember from grade school gym class. On top of it sits my iPod, fifteen thousand songs on a device smaller than a deck of cards.

I stop working. I have to pee. I walk back into the house to the bathroom. My house has a nice bathroom. Nice tile floors, nice bathtub, nice toilet. I think about my craftsmanship on the back door, listening to the sounds of bladder relief, a miniature waterfall in my kingdom. My eyes fall on the medicine cabinet, its door open. Two old orange bottles stare back at me. Oxycontin and codeine, relics from past surgeries to straighten my sinuses and rebuild a recessive gum line. I never used their contents, but yet they travel with me from home to home. It's strange what we keep.

I finish my business, flush the toilet, and walk back through my nice house, past open closet doors and through my kitchen. My nice kitchen with all its amenities of modern life. A row of liquor bottles sit on a shelf. Whiskey, wine, vodka, brandy, the ambrosia of a good time. The drawers and cupboard doors all hang open, not enough to let in light, but too much to be considered closed.

I pick up a piece of cardboard and hold it against the door window, measuring it with my eyes. A pair of scissors make short work of it, cutting it down to size. I slide the piece of cardboard between the glass and the boards. An unnecessary gesture, the tape and glass hold back the cold air as well as the window alone ever did, but I do it anyway. I close the door and shiver again. The furnace barks to life, warming the house, but the garage remains cold. The garage is still a mess. It's the only part of the house that I have not yet organized. Washer, dryer, furnace, hot water heater, modern conveniences in my modern home. A small chest freezer sits along one wall, the wrapped remains of my annual half of beef cocooned within its icy grasp. My bicycle leans on a wall nearby. My tools sit in their box on the floor, good quality tools. A shelf along one side holds camping gear and beer making equipment. Its top shelf is missing, its wood scavenged for other uses.

I look at the blocked window in my newly repaired door and imagine seeing out to my nice patio and backyard. It's dark, but in my mind I can see the high fence and shrubs. The abundant plant life which shields my little oasis from the outside world. It's nice on my patio and in my backyard. It's secluded. It's quiet. When I'm there I can almost forget that I'm in the middle of the city or that any other houses are nearby. It is one of the nicest things about my home, but apparently also a curse.

I close the back door and lock it, then do the same with the door between the kitchen and garage. I walk through my silent house, closing cupboards, drawers, and closet doors. Everything is just where it belongs. Many items have taken short little journeys of inches, but nothing is out of place or missing. I take off my clothes, crawl into bed and breathe a quiet sigh. Whoever they were they had taken their time, they had made sure to go through everything, made sure to look into every nook and cranny. Can you call them a thief if nothing is missing, only disturbed? I feel like I should have more fear or anger, but my mind is numb, only a sense of unease. Would I feel better if they had actually taken something, not just gone through everything? My house is a nice house, but it no longer feels like a home. As I drift off to sleep the words of the police officer echo through my head.

"That's weird."

Feverish Ramblings

I spent a good portion of last night in a feverish stupor, shifting between sweating and shivering, talking philosophy with a dead cat. While I can't complain about the overall quality of the conversation, though it's hard to talk philosophy with someone who insists on referring to you as "little bitch", I don't think that this can be labeled under the category of healthy. Even more disturbing is the fact that I'm pretty sure when the conversation began the cat wasn't dead. This suggests that either the cat expired at some point mid-conversation and I never noticed, or that the cat was faking either its pre or post conversation state.

Now while I certainly do not approve of liars who fake their present condition, somehow that seems preferable to the idea that my verbal sparring partner was able to die mid-debate without me noticing. Either way, all evidence of his existence was gone by the time I woke up in a chilled sweat this morning.

I have the flu. The aches, the pains, the rasping cough, the general feeling of malaise, the whole meal deal. My body is a disgusting battlefield, marred by phlegm and snot, social graces abandoned. Many people are tough when they're sick. They walk tall and hide their disease from the world, their backs unbent, their heads unbowed. No mere tiny virus is enough to ruin their good mood or keep them from doing whatever it is they want to do. I am one of these people, at least in my imagination. In the real world I'm actually extremely pathetic when I'm sick. I lie in my bed, a puddle of man, imagining that the effort it takes me to drag my pestilent carcass to get a drink of water is at least the equal to the effort put forth by the Spartans at Thermopylae. Every task is a heroic endeavor, worthy of orchestrative rendering by Wagner. My fight against my sickness is an epic which will wow people for generations, and be forced reading for bored high school students of a future age.

The greatest quest for a disease ridden body is the venturing forth from the bastion of one's home for supplies. I ease on my clothes and shuffle out the door, my stance and pace suggesting a man in his late nineties instead of a hale man of thirty. My head swims and the whole world seems like an underwater dream. If the drink had brought me to such a state, I would not be allowed to drive, but it's acceptable to do so when I'm sick. I feel like I'm both hungover and high, drifting through the world on a cloud, which occasionally dumps me roughly back to earth with a wracking cough. I'm only half connected with the world. I journey the ten blocks to the local drug store for pain killers, vapor rub, apple juice, and the other weapons needed to fight my internal war.

There are few things as surreal as a residential drug store during the middle of the day. A frantic mother herds her misbehaving children, her eyes empty, dreams forgotten, wondering if anyone would call child services if she paddled her progeny in the parking lot, or if she would even care if someone did. A hobo stands at the counter, muttering to himself as he counts pennies from an old sock to buy a bottle of pop, the clerk looking uncomfortable and wishing he had finished college. An old man raises his voice at the pharmacist, angry over a small clerical error. Inside he feels like the world has failed him, that it hasn't paid him back for the sacrifices of his youth. Even deeper is the fearful knowledge that his body is failing him and his time is growing short. A large fat woman with piercings stands in the makeup aisle, trying on different shades of lip color from sticks she'll never buy. Makeup will not hide her obesity and the sight of her trying shows the power of self-disillusionment. A strange man mutters to himself and rearranges the cracker boxes. A hipster is dropping off pictures to get developed, probably of a neighborhood bridge, probably in black and white. I make my purchases and escape the gauntlet back to my bed, feeling like an observer, a ghost drifting through a world that I'm not a part of.

It only takes a few days of me being sick before my bored brain begins to entertain itself with thoughts of the worse possible futures. I will have to go to the hospital where they will tell me they've never seen a case like mine before. They will panic and put me into some kind of plastic quarantine chamber where they will treat me much like a lab rat, trying to hide their excitement over the medical fame and fortune I represent with an air of professionalism and somberness. My loving family and friends will hold my hand through rubber gloves attached to portholes on the wall of my plastic prison as the doctors take blood samples until my veins collapse. Finally a practitioner with a long face will come in to inform me that there's nothing they can do. He will try to cheer me up by telling me that the new ailment will be named after me, so that any future host can curse me at least indirectly.

With the end certain I prepare myself. I ask for a lawyer and set my last will and testament to paper. My belongings will be separated amongst those I care about most, many of them never knowing how much I cared about them until the end. I bring many of them in one by one and talk for a while, giving them little bits of advice, laughing at old jokes and stories, telling them it will be all right as they hold back tears. Finally I talk with those whom I feel like I must to make my peace with the world, those that I cared for the most, and hurt the most. In silence I hold their hands, still encased in the rubber glove attached to the wall. Nothing more needs to be said or done. I will drift off into the abyss. "A good death," they will say, "a good man."

A pathetic drama, bad enough to make Shakespeare hold his nose and call the whole thing overdone and contrite. In my defense I have been a bachelor the majority of my adult life, a situation which has not led to a large amount of coddling when I'm feeling under the weather. When I get sick I know that I'm the one who's going to have to take care of myself. Even when I had mono, which was about as sick as I've ever been in my life, I took care of myself. I've never liked asking others for help. It's something I've been trying to break myself of, but there is a certain amount of pride in knowing that you don't need other people. That being said, if I choose to act pathetic when I'm sick, but still take care of myself, is it really a bad thing? We're all adults, but who amongst us when we're sick hasn't wanted to be treated like a child again? Who doesn't secretly want to be taken care of?

In all my adult life I can remember someone taking care of me when I was sick only once. I had gotten oral surgery and couldn't talk. A friend came over without being asked and spent the evening with me, watching movies and drinking yogurt milk which she brought, something I had never had before. We communicated via her talking and me writing on a scratchpad. I can't remember ever enjoying myself so much while being sick. I don't know if I ever told her how much her unlooked for act of kindness meant to me.

Anyway, I should probably go back to bed. I'm having trouble making my thoughts orderly or sensible. The healthy world awaits.

Totally Not Abnormal Memories Involving Bulls

For those of you who don't know, I grew up on a cattle ranch. This has left me with a lot of memories that others don't understand. When I was about twelve years old I saw a veterinarian do surgery on a bull's penis. It's a very vivid memory. The twenty-five-hundred pound animal lying on his side, drugged into a deep sleep. The vet, sitting on his knees next to the great black bulk, pulling the bull's member from its sheath. The vet and his scalpel moved quickly, everything had to be finished before the bull started waking up. The careful, precise slices of an artist removed built up scar tissue from the shaft. A needle and thread then quickly sutured the damage before an insanely large amount of gauze and bandages were applied to the wound. The one obvious flaw to the dressing was quickly rectified using a small funnel and a short length of black plastic tubing. The bull soon after awoke, obviously not too happy with the world, and my Dad and I loaded him back into the trailer for the two hour drive home.

Perhaps I need to put the above into context. Bulls, the male bovine, are some of the luckiest bastards on Earth. They are kept by ranchers for one reason, and one reason only. To get their freak on. Every summer the bulls get sent out to live in a verdant green pasture with a personal harem of thirty cows, all of which are just as ready as he is to get down and dirty. What follows is a three month sexfest the likes of which would surely make you grandmother blush, unless you have one of those really dirty grandmothers, then she'd probably just give a knowing wink and some kind of statement about when the boys got back from Europe which would most likely leave you scarred for life. Sometimes a bull would get a harem full of young nubile virgins. Sometimes a harem of doddering old ladies. They never really seemed to care. Bulls love their work.

I could write this whole thing on the mating habits of bulls, but I'll limit myself to the part I always found the funniest. Anytime a bull is in with a group of cows, and one decides it's time to take a piss, the bull immediately sticks his nose in the golden waterfall. He then raises his head, crinkles his nose, and gets a look on his face that can only be described as a combination of dirty old man looking at a girly magazine and fine wine connoisseur sniffing a fancy 1987 Pinot Grigio. Yes, the bull is a filthy dirty pervert. Yes it is gross. But he is doing it for a reason. He is smelling for pheromones that tell him whether or not the cow is in heat.

After he is done with plowing season, the bull spends the next nine months doing nothing but living the good life. He gets to hang out, eat free food, get in scuffles just to prove how badass he is, and receive free medical attention as needed. It's pretty much like you hanging out with your drinking buddies in college. No responsibilities and somebody else footing the bill. Oh yeah, the bulls also screw each other.....a lot. It's less of an attraction thing, and more of an any port in a storm thing. Bulls don't have thumbs or fingers, and it leaves their options during the dry months fairly limited. Anyway, we can leave conversations involving bovine homoeroticism for another time.

To round things up, bulls are stupid. They have a one track mind and this can often times lead to disaster. The bull getting his wang surgically sliced in the first paragraph is a perfect example. That nimrod got himself all hot and heavy over a couple of hot cow asses on the other side of a fence, leading him to decide that he could totally jump his twenty-five-hundred pound body over the aforementioned fence to get his freak on. I should not have to tell you that it is extremely stupid to try to jump a barbed wire fence with your dick hanging out.

Apparently the nimrod bull didn't get the message. Apparently he was the third bull that year to not get the message, hence my Dad's willingness to try experimental penis surgery. Unfortunately the surgery didn't work out, the bull's wang never worked again, and he ended up making lots of hamburger loving children at McDonald's and one chew toy loving dog very happy.

Oh yeah, once a year we also shove a probe up each bull's ass that shocks their prostate until they ejaculate onto a microscope slide so the vet can check their sperm count. Just thought you might like to know.

Waiting

A vivid memory. I'm twelve, sitting in the living room of the house where I grew up. My parents and brothers are gone to a high school basketball game. I didn't want to go. I wasn't feeling well. They allowed me to stay behind. I sit in my father's big easy chair, eating microwave popcorn and watching late night television shows that my mother would have never allowed me to watch. It's the good life. As an adult you forget those early feelings of independence. You forget the thrill of being left to your own devices. The high of having the controls of your life temporarily handed over to you.

The time is 11:00 PM. My parents are late. They should have been home half an hour ago. I look out the window to the long driveway that snakes its way from the main road to the house. My face is reflected back at me, a ghost in the darkness beyond the glass. Any minute the flare of headlights will breach the night, bringing partial detail to an indistinct world. There is nothing. The road is empty. There are lots of reasons to be late. The clock ticks onward, 11:15, 11:30. Still the telltale headlights do not appear. Kernels of doubt begin to expand and pop in my mind.

I get up and pace, decide I'm being silly, and go back to sitting in the easy chair. I get up again, put another piece of wood in the woodstove, and sit back down. They should call if they're going to be late. My mother always harps on me for not calling if I'm going to be late getting home. Why are the rules different for them? They said they'd be back at 10:30. Where are they? More time passes. I fidget. I try to concentrate on just watching television. Still nothing. Where are they?

There has been an accident. The winter weather has made the roads foggy and icy. The car hit a slick patch on the road. It rolled. My parents are hurt. The road is not well traveled. Nobody is going to find them until morning. They're hurt. They're bleeding. They need help. No help is going to come. I need to do something. I need to get in the pickup. I need to drive out and find them. I need to help them.

It doesn't matter. They're already dead. The accident was too severe. They don't survive the initial impact. I'm alone in the world. Completely and utterly alone. They don't let me stay in the house. A twelve year old can't live by himself. I'm shipped off to live with my godparents in the city far away. I survive, but I'm sad. Why did this happen? Why?

Headlights pierce the darkness. Two cones of daylight bouncing down the driveway. The elaborate scenario my mind has created collapses as reality takes back its hold. My parents are fine. I'm fine. I'm not going anywhere. I wipe away the tears that have formed in my eyes. Carefully laid plans are abandoned, no longer needed. I greet my parents as they walk in the door. I don't tell them about my worries, my foolish thoughts. I doubt they would understand.

An Unwanted Gift
Part 1

Her friends tell her she looks like Audrey Hepburn. Even with six hours of alcohol in me it seems quite questionable. The basics are all there; long thick dark hair, pointed chin, large round brown eyes, a pretty smile; but after that the resemblance starts to fail. At the very least the comparison requires a few caveats. It would probably be more fair to describe her as Audrey Hepburn, if Audrey Hepburn had partaken in a few more pastries outside of Tiffany's. This is not to say that she's obese, only that it wouldn't be out of line to describe her as having a little extra. However, to be fair, I've consumed copious amounts of seven and sevens since getting off work, and my sense of the world around me, never mind those related to attraction, most likely are not up to their usual standards.

This is not the where the evening started. No, that location was across the street, but we had been roused from the warm seclusion of that den of inequities by promises of a party. A birthday party for a friend of a friend to be specific. So with high hopes and just a bit of a stagger we bundled up against the chill November air and migrated.

Upon arrival it quickly became apparent that I knew the birthday girl through another friend, but wisely chose not to mention it. The two of them did not get along, but luckily the celebrant did not seem to remember the connection, an oversight I thought best not to point out. In the end such things are not important. Introductions were made, hands were shook, seats were offered and taken. The usual social graces that accompany any merging of two separate parties into one. I was seated next to Hepburn.

I'm at the perfect level of drinking for conversation. The exact point where the booze has released your inhibitions enough to make you unafraid to state the thoughts that blast their way through your mind, but with enough filter still remaining to catch the stray ones that are too offensive or perverse for a public setting. The wonderful point where everything you say is urbane, challenging, and funny. The point of blunt straightforwardness tempered by class. The rules of attraction are complicated, convoluted, and ever changing, but you can always tell when you're winning. It doesn't take much back and forth to tell that I'm winning.

A gust of wind batters itself into the window, a harkening trumpet declaring the start of the holidays. The air outside is cold and sharp, a knife in your lungs when you first walk outside. It would be unfortunate to be alone and cold on a night like this. The trees along the street are dead and bare, only a last few leaves still hanging on to the boughs with a death grip born of desperation. A last reminder of the now gone warmth and happiness of spring and summer. It's the bad times. The season of memories, old joys, heroic deeds, and defeat. The memories of loss, much like the remaining leaves, hang on the hardest.

Pain and tragedy, only a year gone by. No, it's not worth thinking about. Memories do not scar like skin. They are easier to tear open. The world before me, even if imperfect, is better than the world which awaits within my own head. The liquor consumed was meant for its medicinal properties, but the side effects are more than welcome.

A large amount of booze. A willing partner. Pain and regret from the past. All the ingredients needed for one hell of a cocktail. How do these things happen? It's strange, for no matter how many times it does happen, I can never remember clearly how it starts. Confidence, that has to be part of it. It all starts with confidence. The vibe that you know who you are and what you want. The illusion of control over one's own life. I know what's coming. All of the signs are there. A couple of witty remarks, over the top laughter in response, a willingness to work one's way through forced conversation, and the look. The look is the main thing. The look is something that's nearly impossible to describe, but everybody knows it when they see it. The look is what a woman gives a man when she wants him to know she's hooked, that all he needs to do is reel her in, nice and slow. The promise that the game is soon to come to an end. Everyone knows the look, all it takes is the confidence and the want to take advantage of it.

Hepburn is giving me the look. The physical and emotional cocktails sloshing around inside of me make the decision an easy one. My hand moves to her leg. Her hand closes over mine, pushing it higher. Someone makes a suggestion. Was it me or was it her? It doesn't matter. Our addled brains make the decision. The world becomes scattered between point A and B. I find myself in her car, roaring through town on our way to her home in the West Hills. My mind is a mixture of befuddlement and excitement, just beginning to be tinged by the first hints of regret. It's strange to get a taste of the future, to know how the night is going to play out ahead of time. It doesn't matter. It doesn't sway my course. I just don't give a shit.

Her place is a mess. Even in the dark it's easy to tell. Clothes, clean and dirty, strewn across everything. Half eaten pizza from a forgotten age rotting in its open box on the coffee table. Pans with half eaten victuals on the stove. There's nothing here that makes me want to proceed, but it doesn't matter. I've come this far. We've come this far.

She takes me by the hand and leads me back to her bedroom. It's darker. I can't see the filth that is most definitely around me. We proceed with the evening's plan. She presses against me. She consumes me. For a moment it all falls away. We embrace naked, but with our outer layers still intact.

"I have an allergy to latex."

I have to wear a special condom that isn't latex. She has a box in a drawer which she locates with the light from her phone. She helps me put it on, a peremptory move in the right direction. She consumes me again. I feel no passion. It's all just physical need. I don't know how she feels about any of it.

"Hmmmm, you love my big tits, don't you?"

Well endowed women are always making some kind of comment about their tits. It's a feature they can't seem to get past. A totem they hope will forgive all other shortcomings. A simplistic view of man at his most carnal and basic, born of the days of adolescent madness and hungry eyes. I had a friend in college who loved big tits. He loved them to the point that he'd ignore everything else about a girl, perpetuating the cycle. I'm not like him.

Pumping. Hands gripping my backside. The house is warm. Too warm. I sweat heavily. The evaporation carries off the last vestiges of my inebriation. It's frightening to sober up at such a moment. To look down and see a stranger. Someone that you feel nothing for. No attraction, physical or mental. I don't care about this woman. She could die tomorrow and it would have no impact on my life. I go limp. I pull out. I murmur an excuse about too much whiskey, roll over, and go to sleep. She tries to cuddle. I let her, but I wish she wouldn't.

When the morning sun peaks in the window we barely speak. The bedroom is just as much of a disaster as the living room. There are no pleasantries. There is no exchange of numbers. I have her drive me back to my car before the warming orb has a chance to climb above the trees. It's an uncomfortable ride, I can sense it. Both of us are left wondering what the fuck happened. We arrive. I get out and unlock my car. She drives off into the morning mist. I'm glad to see her go.

My Guide To Initial Messages While Online Dating Part 2

You know it's just a matter of time. You can call it quits, but the siren song will draw you back in again. They say there are many fish in the sea, but there is no fishing hole quite so filled to the brim as online dating. Sure, you've never caught anything in those teeming waters, but you have heard of people who have. If they can do it, why not you? All it takes is a little patience, time, and just a teensy bit of charm. In the end loneliness and lust overcome all doubts. So it was that I returned to the countless profiles of online dating, ready to further refine my skills in creating the ever elusive perfect initial message.

Attempt #18: RockStarGoddess

After combing through numerous profiles to find the perfect
woman to mark the restarting of my quest, I soon grew
overwhelmed and settled on just selecting someone attractive,
though not so attractive that I thought them out of my league.
The selected woman's profile was all over the place, so I
strategically decided to shotgun a whole bunch of comments at
her at once to see if any would stick. She mentioned in her
profile that she only wanted "real" people to contact her, which I
felt fit me pretty well. She also had some strange comments
regarding Bohemian fabric and the movie *Melancholia*.

*This might seem a silly question, but I don't have any idea what
would be considered Bohemian fabric? For some reason I
picture it having to do with the philosopical Bohemians, not the
Czech ones.*

*Also, please rest assured that I am real. I did go through a short
phase of wondering if I was just a figment of my cat's
imagination, but the cat died and I'm still here, so that theory
was shot pretty full of holes.*

Shawn

*P.S. Relax, I have it on good authority that Melancholia is going
to miss the Earth. Though I have noticed a lot of symbolic slow
motion sequences taking place recently.*

I never got to find out what the hell Bohemian fabric is.
RockStarGoddess didn't send back any kind of response, which
unfortunately for me, kicked off a serious existential crisis where
I wondered if I was truly just a figment of my dead cat's
imagination.

Attempt #19: Olivialive

They say that one of the best ways to get someone's attention is to create a bridge of commonality, show them that the two of you share similar values and experiences, thus giving you something to talk about. However, sometimes a profile has little to nothing in it, which in turn forces one to look for things in common that in the grand scheme of things don't really mean shit. A good example of this would be my second attempt, a woman who had little to offer about herself other than the fact that she was taller than average and tired of people mentioning it all the time. Being a tall man myself, it seemed a perfect fit.

I as well have never been able to figure out why people feel the need to mention how tall I am. It's not like I never noticed before. Their next question always inevitably seems to be whether or not I play basketball. Its too bad that tallism is so rampant in our society. Maybe we need to have a parade or something?

My brother, who is even taller, once had a random lady in the grocery store ask him how tall he was. He returned with asking how much she weighed. She got mad and told him that some things are just rude to ask. He said, "exactly." Unfortunately his point seemed to go right over her head.

Crap now I'm making tall jokes. I'm going to wrap this up before the poor puns get out of hand.

Shawn

Few things bring people together quite like suffering from the same prejudice. Olivialive replied and over time our mutual hatred of people who feel the need to point out the obvious grew our bond until we both felt comfortable actually meeting in person. Unfortunately, that's when things took a turn for the worst. As it turns out, you can't really build a relationship just off of both being taller than average.

Attempt #20: Sophiebpbp
The success of actually getting a date after just two initial messages probably went to my head more than it should have. Maybe that's why I felt cocky enough to fully let my freak flag fly. Sophiebpbp's profile claimed she had the best job in the universe. I don't remember exactly what it was, maybe a teacher or jazzercise instructor or something, but my boundless imagination really doubted it was true. I might have completely skipped over her profile, which also mentioned that she enjoyed card games, if it hadn't been for what appeared to be a good sense of humor. She joked that she liked watching street fights, so I thought, what the hell, might as well not hold back.

I'm afraid I must disagree with you. The best job in the universe is being the personal lion tamer for Teddy Roosevelt. But since Teddy is long dead I will concede that your job may possibly be the best job in the universe currently.

I personally find street fights to be a little old hat. These days I'm into more current crazes like underground Kangaroo boxing.

Shawn

P.S. I'll take you in cards any day of the week, except Bridge. Despite the newspaper printing Bridge tips every week, I have no interest in playing.

I didn't hear anything back from her, though this was probably only because of a severe bout of depression brought on by her realizing that her job actually wasn't the best one in the universe. Either that or perhaps the only card game she liked was Bridge.

Attempt #21: Urbanbambi
Time to be a little honest about things. I'm attracted to crazy. I know it's not healthy and that at times it can even be dangerous, but for whatever reason nothing gets my motor running quite like someone slightly off their rocker. That's probably why I decided that it would be a good idea to send a message to a woman whose profile made a point of bragging that she still had all of her fingers and toes, and then went on to demand that any man who messaged her had to be able to carry her with little to no effort if her legs fell off due to leprosy. However, the cherry on top of the crazy sundae had to be the fact that she included a link on her profile to her brother's profile. I'm not sure what the point of that was. It's not like I'd be looking at her profile and suddenly just change my mind and decide that I wanted to date dudes.

Congratulations on having all of your fingers and toes. I was going to write more but then got strangely caught up in reading your brother's profile to see if he was as hilarious as you described. Now I'm a little rushed so I can get to bed at a decent hour.

Shawn

P.S. I am willing to carry your legless leprous body for a mile if your legs made up a significant portion of your body weight and you agree that if we ever get involved at a chicken fight at the pool, I get to be on top.

There's nothing crazy likes quite like crazy. While she sent a message back, it was mostly to quiz me on her brother's profile

to prove that I actually hadn't read it. Questions I easily answered given that I only claim to do things if I've actually done them. Our messages back and forth then broke down into negotiations which ended with me giving up being the top rung in a chicken fight to the guarantee of always getting to be the wheelbarrow in any unplanned wheelbarrow races.
Unfortunately it was all for naught, for she soon after broke off communication.

Attempt #22: CAP84
Anytime a woman says she loves herself some Jack Handy, the delightful advice giver from old Saturday Night Live episodes, you know I'm going to try and make a move. That's just good old fashioned common sense. That being said, I felt it was important to try and clarify exactly what kind of person she was looking for given that her profile explicitly stated that certain types of people should not try to contact her.

My favorite Jack Handy is as follows (please excuse the paraphrasing):

"When you're a child walking to school there is nothing worse then getting splashed by a passing car hitting a puddle. You stand there, wondering if you should go to school sodden and wet, or go home to change and be late for school. So while the kid was sitting there wondering, I drove by and splashed him again."

......

And crap, I've just wasted a half hour reading Jack Handey quotes, many of which are better then the one I thought was my favorite.

Shawn

P.S. I once did play dead at a business meeting, unfortunately nobody noticed.

P.P.S. Is it all right to message you if your both good company and a bathroom stall type of good time?

Mysteriously I never heard back from her. I'm guessing CAP84 was just saying that she was a Jack Handy fan in a lame attempt to sound cool. Pretty pathetic on her part if you ask me. As a side note, I have absolutely no memory what the hell the whole thing with playing dead in a business meeting was about.

Attempt #23: LittleLimaBee

A woman who claims that she might accidentally start the Norse apocalypse. Of course I'm going to message her. Someone who thinks people who drive hybrid cars are assholes. Even better. A member of the fairer sex who loves the novels of Douglas Adams. Christmas has come early. Now how in the hell do I impress her?

So, your friends say that you are the most likely person to start an apocalypse, and then you take a "Mythological Profile" test and get Jormungand. Your friends might be onto something there.

I was reading a study the other day, and by that I mean reading an article on a humor website that cited a study, that had some statistical data showing that people who drive hybrid cars are less courteous compared to the average driver. The theory is that since they see themselves doing a good deed, it becomes easier for them to justify being less courteous (i.e. I'm saving the world, so forgetting to use my blinker is really no big deal). Maybe it works the same way for bikers.

Shawn

P.S. Forty-two is the exact number of minutes that the average diner will wait before they go from, "when you have a second," to, "holy shit where the hell is my food." It is unknown if this is related to the mathematics involved in splitting a restaurant check.

Believe it or not the above words pulled straight out of my ass somehow worked. Apparently women just can't resist a knowledgeable man willing to talk about the end of the world and why people are sometimes jackasses. Unfortunately, that's as far as it got. After a couple of messages back and forth things petered out. Back to the drawing board.

Attempt #24: Hello_Panda
In her profile Hello_Panda mentioned that she enjoyed sniffing laundry detergent. Now most people would find that a little weird, but I've just kind of learned to roll with things since I'm a little weird myself.

Sniffing the laundry detergent makes a lot of sense. Nobody wants all of their clothes to smell like something unpleasant. I'm going to start doing it. If anybody asks me why I'm sniffing all of the detergent's in the store, I'll just go all crazy eyed and tell them its to get high.

Please don't take this to be rude, I don't know and I'm just curious, but what does a Geography major write a thesis about?

Shawn

P.S. I also like sharing dishes at restaurants so I can try more things. Though I've learned its better to ask people before I do it.

She didn't answer, but I imagine she was having a pretty rough time when she realized that nobody in their right mind would ever read a Geography thesis. Either that or she was too busy trying to get high on laundry detergent.

Attempt #25: LsOm

Things started to go downhill at this point. One failure after another cut down my faith in the idea that I would ever meet somebody. Depression began to set in, which of course led to drinking, which as one can easily imagine, led to overly philosophical messages.

Like many things in life I think wine and friends are on a sliding scale. The higher the quality of the drinking partners, the more I'm willing to put up with poor quality wine. Conversely, the higher the quality of the wine, the more I'm willing to put up with poor quality company. To have both good wine and good friends in one sitting, now that's just a good thing.

LsOm must have assumed that I had access to really high quality wine. I never heard a peep out of her.

Attempt #26: SparklingLava

Perhaps it was the drink that convinced me it would be a good idea to message a woman who stated in her profile that what she was really looking for was an open relationship with Amy Poehler and Will Arnett. I hated having to be the one to break the bad news to her, but on the plus side, it gave me a pretty solid opening. SparklingLava's profile also stated that she hated hipsters because they always felt the need to show off how they knew the names of more obscure bands than she did.

I'm sorry to have to be the one to tell you, but Amy Poehler and Will Arnett are breaking up. You could probably still get involved in an open relationship with them, but it would probably be fairly awkward. I imagine a lot of snide comments, though the sex would probably be pretty good.

Wow, when I go back and read the last paragraph that's a terrible way to start a conversation. But in all honesty these kind of things run through my head quite a bit, so I'm just going to leave it.

Also, if you get involved in a who's heard of more bands conversation, couldn't you just start making up band names, I mean, who's really going to know.

I never got a reply, but I wasn't all that surprised. Who has time to message some online dolt when you're busy buying tickets to Hollywood so you can hook up with Amy and/or Will? I can't really blame her. We all have to follow our dreams. Also, initial messages are probably not the best time for introspection.

Attempt #27: Bluflame9732

I tried to take this one at least a little seriously given that Bluflame9732's profile made her seem like a pretty nice woman. She was originally from Vermont and liked to play scrabble. She seemed like the kind of genuine person you'd have no second thoughts about taking to meet your parents.

I know that its probably blasphemous to a person from Vermont, but for some reason I've always preferred the fake maple syrup. I don't know why. I've tried countless different real maple syrups, driven by the idea that I should like the real more then the fake, but its no good. Maybe its because that's what we always had when I was a kid. King corn got me young.

On a different note, I'm probably not better at scrabble. I'm not saying that I have a poor vocabulary. But I seem to have a bad habit of drawing mostly vowels whenever I play. My strategy largely consists of waiting until someone puts down a really high scoring word, and then putting a "S" on the end.

I got a reply, but it was mostly just to call me a blasphemer for not using real maple syrup. I was a little disappointed. It's not every day I just give away my winning scrabble strategies.

Attempt #28: Seren_K
My introspective state just seemed to get worse with every message. While one should never lie when writing initial messages, filtering yourself somewhat is probably not a bad idea. Before letting people know that you're just a little nuts, you need to give them a chance to get to know your better qualities that make putting up with the rest worthwhile. Unfortunately, I didn't do any of that and my messages just kind of collapsed into spouting out the first thing that came to mind. Seren_K's profile claimed that she had a really thick Minnesota accent that she was trying to hide. She also stated that two big factors she was looking for in a prospective mate were that they didn't care about getting yellow lab hair on black pants and that they had their shit together.

If I was you I'd quit trying to shake the Minnesota accent and instead just ham it up to an extreme that can only be described as awkward for everyone around you.

Anyways, I should probably not just write the first thing that pops into my head on these things, but it seems like the most honest thing to do. The whole thing with the yellow lab hair on black pants seems pretty specific. Have you had trouble with that before?

Also, please rest assured that I have my shit together. I eat a lot of fiber so this has never been a problem. This seems like something really personal to wonder about people though.

No replay, though I wasn't really all that disappointed. The Minnesota accent has to be one of the least sexy of accents.

Attempt #29: Hufflepie

The next profile that caught my eye included a triple exposure picture where it looked like three of Hufflepie were sitting at a restaurant booth having a conversation. I thought it was a pretty creative profile picture, so of course I wanted to let her know my appreciation through my own creativity.

You on the left in your third picture down does not seem very interested in what you on the right is saying. She just has that look like she wishes she was anywhere else. At least middle you is pretending to pay attention, even though she's actually just wondering if its too early to order a third beer and why you on the right is being so serious.

I never heard back from her. Maybe I was mistaken and Hufflepie was really one of a set of triplets.

Attempt #30: Red_Gemini

As my frustration with the whole online dating process grew, my messages began to get shorter and shorter. I was getting tired of putting in a huge amount of effort with little to no reward. The quality of things that attracted me also seemed to decline at an alarming rate. For instance, what caught my eye in this woman's profile was the claim that she was good at pretending to be Kristen Wiig and putting her foot in her mouth.

So wait.....are the pretending to be Kristin Wigg and putting your foot in your mouth dependent on each other, or independent of each other. If their dependent on each other you might have the makings of a great stage act.

Was I successful? Nope. However, I still think her combined talents would've made for one hell of a great stage act.

Attempt #31: Squarerootofneg1

After several short messages I managed to perk myself up enough to put some effort back into it. Unfortunately, perusing through the various profiles, I probably let the pendulum swing back too far the other way. Squarerootofneg1 seemed nice. Maybe too nice. Her comments mostly were based around the book she was reading and the fact that she disliked texting. It kind of seemed like the profile your mother would put up.

Congratulations on avoiding the use of emoticons. I've always found them annoying and have avoided using them as much as possible. I don't really like texting either, though the ever moving tide of societal norms has forced me to accept it as a general part of my day to day life. Granted, a large part of my anti-text stance is probably due to my stubborn refusal to upgrade from my current flip phone.

I'm a one book at a time kind of person myself, but I can understand the allure of being able to switch them out. Sorry to hear the non-fiction is always getting neglected. I feel like there's a lot of poorly written non-fiction out there, which is too bad, because a lot of the stories are really interesting. I just got done with a non-fiction about a cult called the Holy Rollers that was in Corvallis back in 1905. It was really well written and kept me pretty captivated.

Did I get a reply? Hell yeah I got a reply. The drought was finally over, at least for a little while. We messaged back and forth for a bit, but it didn't really go anywhere, probably because in many ways Squarerootofneg1 was just boring as shit, or not crazy if you prefer, which really puts more of the onus on me. On another note, you should really learn more about that sex cult in Corvallis, Oregon back in 1905. That shit was nuts.

Attempt #32: Ktt_486
I was getting close to giving up on the whole online dating thing, but before I did, I decided to throw up a Hail Mary pass of bluntness. A declaration to the world, or at least to one poor woman in it, that here I am, crazy and all.

Hello fellow tall person. I will openly admit that I'm becoming kind of bored with this OkCupid thing and I'm pretty much now just writing messages to entertain myself in some kind of weird experiment to see whether or not people will respond. Strangely enough my response rate has not really decreased any, but the dates I have gone on have gotten more entertaining.

You claim to be a creative swearer, a quality I take great pride in myself exhibiting, lets hear what you got.

Also I noticed that the six things you could never do without rearranged a little bit make a nice little story about two people hooking up. Friends, hugs, exercise, orgasms, purpose, good sleep.

Believe it or not, but this actually worked. I got a reply, but soon after Ktt_486 closed her account. So yeah, that was a first. Also, creative swearer my ass.

Attempt #33: Wanderlustforlyf
It was the end of the line for me. I couldn't do it anymore. The whole experience of online dating was too draining to keep it up. However, like any great athlete, I decided to give it my all in one last desperate attempt. The last lucky woman's profile said that she wanted to hang out with a mostly nice person who would get a little tipsy and converse with her. There was no doubt in my mind that I could easily meet such qualifications.

I am mostly a nice person who enjoys getting moderately tipsy with strangers. As evidence that I'm a nice guy I have never had a picture taken showing off my abs or standing next to a really cool car. As for the part about getting tipsy, you'll just have to take my word on it.

Talking with total strangers can sometimes be weird because you never know what subjects are going to interest them, so for the sake of efficiency here are some subjects I could cover over a few beers:

1) What your original hair color was. I'm a good guesser.
2) What is the answer to 6 down.
3) Points in life that make you feel relatively old.
4) What the people on the date across the room are probably saying.
5) The current socio-economic issues in China.
6) Tales from my abnormal childhood on a large cattle ranch in the middle of nowhere.

7) The sorta creepy fact that OkCupid is kind of like shopping on Amazon.
8) What the hell is going to happen on Game of Thrones
9) What happens when we die?
10) A multitude of random fun facts.

With the last of my strength I strived for the goal, and fell far short. I never heard anything back from Wanderlustforlyf. Perhaps I should have included some abs pictures. It was the end of the line. I couldn't do it anymore. I accepted that perhaps I was destined to be alone, or if not, my partner in crime wasn't to be found on the worldwide web. I shut off my profile once again, though I did not delete it. One never knows what the future might hold.

Pineappaphilia

"Hey, there you are. Sorry I'm late."

"No problem."

"Just got a little caught up. Had someone call me just when I was leaving."

"Don't worry about it."

"This seems like a pretty nice place."

"Oh yeah, it's a great place, one of the best pizza places in town."

"Really?"

"Naw, but it's hard to beat how convenient it is."

"Has the waitress been coming around regular? I'm starving."

"She's a little slow, but don't worry, I already ordered."

"You did?"

"Yeah, I figured you'd be late, so I went ahead and ordered a large."

"What the hell man? You couldn't just wait?"

"Well, maybe if you showed up on time for once this wouldn't be an issue."

"Motherfucker."

"Relax."

"Fuck."

"Calm down. I ordered your favorite."

"Do you even know what my favorite pizza is?"

"Yeah, after three years of friendship I don't have any idea what your favorite pizza is. I've just been totally oblivious to everything about you. Christ, just relax, I got pineapple and Canadian bacon."

"Okay. Okay. I'm sorry man. You do know me."

"Damn straight I do. Just relax. I know you like pineapple."

"Like it, fuck it, I love pineapple. It's the only topping that belongs on a pizza. My mouth is watering just thinking about it."

"Whoa, whoa, calm down there buddy, we're in a public place."

"Sorry, I just really like pineapple."

"Yeah. I bet you do."

"Yeah, I do."

"Maybe you should see a therapist about this."

"What the hell are you talking about?"

"C'mon man, it's all well and good having a favorite food, but you gotta be careful not to take it too far."

"What?"

"I just don't want to walk into the grocery store one day and see you in the produce section all sweaty and worked up."

"What the fuck are you talking about?"

"You know, all horned up, muttering to yourself, pawing all the pineapples until a store clerk gets up the guts to ask you to leave."

"What the fuck is wrong with you? God, you're weird."

"I don't think a sweaty man who's trying to hide his pineapple induced boner has any right to judge other people's fallacies."

"How would you even fuck a pineapple?"

"I don't know. I guess I just kind of assumed you were shoving them up your ass or something."

"That doesn't sound physically possible. I mean hell, the pineapple to sphincter ratio is way off."

"Yeah, I guess it wouldn't work."

"Even if it did, wouldn't all the spines hurt like hell?"

"I kind of assumed that was part of the draw. At the very least the tops would make them easy to remove."

"Gross."

"I don't know, maybe pineapple fuckers cut them up before they fuck them."

"That doesn't make a lot of sense. I think a whole pineapple would be preferable."

"I don't know, the sliced pineapple has holes."

"No, think about it. The pineapple is a sexy fruit. On the outside its all spiney and tough, on the inside sweet and moist. It's like the perfect analogy for every woman I've ever been attracted to."

"How the hell would you even fuck a whole pineapple?"

"Maybe pineapple fuckers have some kind of coring device."

"Coring device?"

"Yeah, you know, some kind of fruit corer to make a hole in the pineapple. You know, to stick your dick in."

"That could probably work. But aren't pineapples fairly acidic? Wouldn't it burn the shit out of your pee hole?"

"I guess I was just kind of assuming that would be part of the draw."

"So all pineapple fuckers are a little masochistic then?"

"Between the acid burned urethras and carrying around a fruit corer all the time I just kind of assumed that would be the case."

"It must be awkward for your wife, going to the store with you, watching you nearly lose control."

"She's pretty understanding, she just wants me to be happy. Besides, I feel like out of all the sweaty men in the produce aisle, pineapple fucking guy is pretty far up the ladder of respectability."

"I don't know. What about all the phallic shaped vegetable lovers?"

"Fucking amateurs. Being a pineapple fucker means really committing to a fetish. Think about it. Pineapple fuckers have to go out and buy a special stainless steel pineapple corer."

"Couldn't it be plastic?"

"No, it's well known that the best pineapple corers are stainless steel, very spendy, but they last longer. You don't want to be getting all heated up for some lusty pineapple loving just to have your corer break."

"That would suck."

"Also you have to make sure the corer is the right width and that it goes the right depth to maximize your pineapple loving experience."

"Shit, a guy with a pineapple fetish is damn near royalty compared to some random dude shoving radishes up his ass."

"Shoving radishes up his ass? What the fuck?"

"Yeah radishes, they're nature's butt plugs."

"That's an image I didn't need man."

"Hey, it popped into my head, somebody had to share the horror."

"Thanks."

"Where do you think you'd even get a pineapple corer?"

"I don't know."

"It's definitely something you wouldn't want to buy in a store. There is literally no way to look classy when you're in line at the checkout counter with a fucking corer. You could be the guy who cured cancer, but in everyone else's' eyes you'd just be that dude who is probably fucking pineapples when he gets home."

"Yeah, it's definitely an Amazon type purchase. Nothing but a nice square box. Nobody has to know that you're a filthy filthy pineapple loving pervert."

"God I'd love to read the reviews for that item."

"You are a sick man my friend."

"Hey, I'm not the one with the secret pineapple fetish."

"Enough already."

"It's okay man, I'm your friend, I'll accept you as you are. Just come out of the fruit stand already."

"You're getting a little loud."

"Your friends and wife all care about you. We'll accept you as you are. Just admit that you're a pineapple fucker. It will be just like a Lifetime movie."

"What, it's a movie now?"

"Yeah, just imagine. The movie starts with your wife not knowing you're a pineapple fucker. She thinks you two are just a nice suburban couple with everything going for them. Nice house, nice car, good jobs, perfect life. The only thing that's kind of weird is she notices that you seem to go through a lot of pineapples. However, things are good so she shrugs it off, just figures you're a guy who really loves eating pineapple. Then she begins to get a little suspicious that something is up. She finds a couple of your cored and loved pineapples in the recycling bins. You avoid questions about them. Then while looking for batteries one day she finds your corer in your desk drawer. Again she confronts you, and again you make excuses for what it's for."

"Makes sense, lots of uses for a pineapple corer."

"Yeah, though one with a gilded handle is kind of weird. Anyway, finally one night you don't show up to a friend's birthday party like you agreed to and your wife comes home earlier than expected to catch you fucking a pineapple. She freaks out."

"Undoubtedly."

"You try to explain to her that it's not what she thinks, but she can't calm down. She leaves the house to stay with friends. After a couple of days you finally get her to talk to you and you explain how you slowly fell into the world of pineapple humping. She agrees to move back in as long as you never fuck another pineapple again."

"You just can't quit pineapple fucking cold turkey."

"Hell no. At first you're all right, you try your best to keep your promise, you love your wife, but then it slowly starts to get weird. You start looking at pineapple pictures online. You start having problems getting turned on by your wife. You even try experimenting with other produce items. Finally everything comes to a head when she sends you to the store with a grocery list that includes pineapples. As you go into the produce aisle you begin to sweat profusely, your hands and eyes begin to twitch, it's been so long. You completely lose control and you get arrested in the parking lot, fucking a pineapple in your car."

"Fuck."

"Your wife bails you out, she loves you so much. She decides that if accepting you as you are is the only way to have you in her life, then she'll do it. She lets you start fucking pineapples again. She even buys a pineapple suit to wear for when the two of you make love. But she's not happy, she wants to be treated like a woman, not like a pineapple."

"Dude, fucking keep it down."

196

"You're not happy either, because you can tell she's not happy and that your fetish has completely taken control of not only your life, but also hers. Finally you agree to go into treatment to save your marriage. You're voluntarily committed and when normal therapy methods don't work you agree to the extreme measure of electroshock therapy. This part will have several powerful scenes of you being shocked while your wife watches and cries. Finally after all that, the doctor's happily declare that you're cured. You go home to a big welcome back party at your house. The last shot of the film is of all the partygoers in the front room while you're standing alone in the dining room, staring down at your welcome home cake.

"Yeah?"

"It's a pineapple upside down cake."

"Fuck man. Jesus fucking Christ."

"You haven't even heard the best part."

"The best part?"

"Yeah, the best part. All of the trailers for the movie will make it look like it's a nice family movie about the adventures of a spunky cartoon rabbit and his squirrel friend. Then the first scene of the movie starts....bam.....you fucking a pineapple."

"That's really fucked up."

"It's fucking awesome."

"What the fuck is wrong with you?"

"Probably a lot. Oh sweet, the pizza's here."

"......"

"Dig in."

"I'm not hungry."

An Unwanted Gift
Part 2

"I don't think I can do this. I can't deal with this."

We stare at each other. She is right next to me on the couch. The couch where I had taken her for the first time. Her hand rests in mine. The last bit of contact between us. She had wanted more when she swept in the door, but I had stopped her. It had to be done. I feel as though she's shouting to me from the other side of a great chasm. I don't know what to say. Her face remains stony and emotionless, but all held inside escapes through the windows to her soul, the weak points in the wall that she has thrown up. In her eyes I see pain, sadness, regret, and a yearning for a better answer. I know my eyes are mirror images of her own. The same emotions creating one last bridge between us.

The silence in my apartment is deafening. Every creak as the house settles is the scream of a banshee. The heating vents thrum with intensity as they labor to push back the early February cold which crawls through the windows. I know I should say something. I know I should fight. My mind struggles for the better answer that she needs. Something that will keep everything from falling apart. There's still a chance. The army of my heart marches in formation, girded for battle, but I have nothing. No tactics. No strategy. No hope. Fight after fight. Defeat after defeat. A steady retreat with no victories. How can one know how to get what they've never experienced? I don't have the morale to fight another battle. There's a tear falling down her cheek. I reach up to brush it away, but she pulls back. It's all crumbling away.

I don't agree to go on many blind dates. People in relationships are always trying to play matchmaker. There's something about a relationship that makes those involved want to be peddlers of the drug called love to their poor single friends. It's usually best to ignore such offers, to make polite talk and quickly change the subject. There's a certain level of desperation to blind dates, a feeling of giving up. Whenever I think of blind dates I always remember the statement made by the intermediary of one of my first.

"I think you'll be good for her. You're not like her last boyfriend, you have a job and a car with all of its doors."

Such statements have more red flags than a May Day parade. It goes without saying that it didn't go well. Disastrous is a more descriptive word.

Katy hadn't been like that. I only agreed to it because the offer was put forward by someone I trusted, plus I had fallen to that level of desperation. My own fumblings had resulted in the faltering of my confidence to the point that I no longer trusted my own ability to change my relationship status. It was easier to let someone else take the wheel. It had all been so simple to arrange. Both of us showed up to the same movie night surrounded by mutual friends. Both of us knew it was a setup. Both of us only going along with it to appease a friend's insistent demands. It's funny to go into things expecting to be disappointed and instead finding yourself pleasantly surprised. It's strange to discover that maybe your friend does know you well enough to make correct assumptions about what you're looking for. It's curious for the other person to feel the same.

First dates are always awkward. They're especially awkward when you discover the coffee shop that you carefully selected is in fact not open on Sunday. There are literally hundreds of coffee shops within the city limits, yet still it takes twenty minutes of frantic driving to find another. Rushing from block to block, texting updates to a soon to arrive date. The coffee shop had been her idea. I usually prefer to meet in bars for a couple of beers. She doesn't drink a lot of beer. I don't drink coffee at all. It had seemed like a fair compromise. Location is not that important.

It had been a good first date. Scratch that. A great first date. Sometimes on first dates you just sit in awkward silence. Sometimes they're nothing but questions which would seem more appropriate for a job interview. This date had a bit of both, with a nice smattering of jokes and random topics of conversation thrown in the mix. An enjoyable first date is one of the nicest things in the world. The act of talking to someone and, much to your mutual surprise, discovering that four hours have passed by. On a cold Sunday afternoon I made out with her next to her car as the patrons of a barbeque joint looked on.

The second date follows the first, and the third follows the second. One step at a time as you move forward. You get swept away in such things, reveling in the ingestion of a drug like no other known. Getting to know someone, both of you letting out small parts of who you truly are. Slowly pulling down the walls that you have put up. Gradually letting out secret regrets and joys. Shedding layers to show the whole person beneath. The fertilization of the tiny sapling, so fragile that neither of you dare directly verbalize the dream of it growing into a mighty oak. These are the things that intimacy are made of. This is what it takes to feel whole.

Of course as each explores the mental canvas of the other, you also begin to explore the hidden world of the physical as well. Passion, heat, and yearning. We are all born with physical needs given to us by millennia of evolution. A hunger that can only be satiated by another's flesh. The trick is to find someone who can fulfill both your physical and mental needs. Kissing leads to groping, groping leads to dry humping. You know the rest. Passions boil over and the wants of the body overcome the doubts of the mind. The outer shells of fabric are tossed aside and we become the providers of each other's pleasure. On the couch, in the bed, on the counter, in the shower, anywhere will do.

The relationship eventually reaches a magical point. A place where the two of you tame the physical needs of the body and then walk through the city hand in hand. You have no particular destination in mind. You're just glad to be with each other. You stop at a likely looking restaurant, eat a nice dinner, lounge and laugh, then return home to continue your carnal explorations. Hormones course through your bodies, a natural high designed to get people past their doubts, insecurities, and worries long enough to possibly build a real relationship.

They look like zits. Small red bumps with pearly heads. I count thirty-six across my shaft and testicles. I sit alone and naked in a hotel room in Kansas. I noticed them for the first time earlier that day. In the middle of a business meeting I excused myself to use the bathroom. Stepping up to the urinal I found them staring up at me. Shock and disgust. Horror and fear. What the hell was this? What the fuck were they? It goes without saying that I was not very productive for the rest of the day.

I type frantically at the computer, searching for pictures to try and figure out what is going on. My mind is in a frenzy as I search, stopping at likely images to compare them with my own malady. It's not an easy task. The pictures are almost always of the symptoms at their worst. Herpes. Is it herpes? Maybe it's just some kind of rash. Could it really be something so benign? What about these which I've never heard of before? What's happening? Panic sets in and I don't know what to do. I have a wealth of knowledge at my fingertips, but I lack the ability to either dash my hopes that it's nothing or ignore my fears that it's the worst of so many possibilities. My attempts at self-diagnosis only lead me into a tailspin of anxiety which makes rational thought impossible.

I'm not alone here. I have a friend attending college nearby. It's only with great reluctance that I ask for the help that I desperately need. My face burns red when the words escape my lips. We were just supposed to go out and get drinks. Plans change. The afternoon of the day after my discovery he drives me to a walk-in clinic. I try to make jokes, anything to cover how much anxiety I feel, but it alleviates nothing. At the clinic I fill out forms and then we sit in silence, a chair empty between us as is protocol between those of the male gender. Every second seems to take a minute. An hour turns into two and a half days. The nurse finally calls me back to an examination room. The usual follows. Weight, temperature, heart rate, blood pressure, then down to business. It's awkward to explain such an intimate problem to a stranger. It's even more awkward to take down your pants to show them. The nurse hmms and hahs as she handles my junk in a professional manner. She marks a few things on a sheet and then leaves.

More waiting, but now I'm alone. Not even the comforting silence of an uncomfortable friend. At the very least the waiting room has magazines to read. Here there is nothing except a poster about prostate exams. Once when I was younger I got bored and started going through all the countless drawers, not looking for anything, just curious. The doctor had walked in, leading to a fairly awkward exchange. I do nothing this time. I just sit on my little table covered in paper in silence.

When the doctor finally comes in she asks many of the same questions as the nurse. Again I have to awkwardly describe the problem. Again I lower my pants and allow my junk to be professionally handled by cold hands encased in rubber gloves. She takes notes, types on her computer, and gives the situation some thought.

"Folliculitis."

The declaration is full of self-confidence. Relief surges through me. Folliculitis. Clogged sweat glands. It was one of the more benign things I had come across during my attempts at self-diagnosis. I'm going to have to buy my friend a few beers to celebrate. The doctor is still talking. She's filling out a prescription.

"Be sure to have your own doctor examine them when you get home."

You would think that a doctor in a university town would have a vast knowledge of sexually transmitted diseases. You would think they would recognize one when they saw it.

"Molluscum contagiosum."

My doctor's declaration has the same air of authority as that of the doctor's in Kansas. The relief of the past couple days collapses. I feel myself deflate, my spirit and soul retracting until my skin is several sizes too big. It was supposed to be just a routine visit. A quick confirmation of the diagnosis. It's none of these things. It's a nightmare. The doctor roots through a drawer, hands me a pamphlet, and walks out of the room.

Molluscum contagiosum. A virus that lives on the skin that's related to chickenpox. It causes a zit like structure to form on the skin. Spread by skin to skin contact. Common in children and as a sexually transmitted disease. Incubation period before the first symptoms appear can range as long as six months. Only infectious when the bumps are present, but easy to spread to others and to re-infect yourself when they are. If untreated can last for a year or more. I sit alone and try not to cry. Molluscum contagiosum. I've never heard of it before, but now it's mine. I can feel tears forming at the corners of my eyes, but I choke them back as the doctor re-enters. She advises that we start treatment immediately. I of course agree.

I lay on my back on the paper covered table. My pants are off and my shirt is pulled up, exposing my disease ridden genitalia for all the world to see. The doctor stands over me holding a strange and very medical looking gun. She moves the gun to each of the bumps and hits it with a concentrated blast of liquid nitrogen. It burns. God how it burns. With each blast my hands tighten around the edge of the table.

"The liquid nitrogen doesn't actually kill the virus, it just induces a quicker immune response."

The doctor is matter of fact about her work.

"Most people only have us do ten or so at a time because of the pain."

It's a terrible pain, but there are things that are worse.

"Do them all."

Thirty-six bumps. Thirty-six blasts of liquid nitrogen. Her hands prod and shift, hunting out targets. Each spot that is treated leaves behind an area of white discoloration. The doctor assures me that it will fade. She comments on how tough I am. I try my best to hide how watery my eyes have become. It takes less than half an hour.

"Some will likely pop back up. Come back in three weeks."

Katy continues to stare at me and I continue to stare at her. She has shown no signs of infection and is unlikely to get any since this is the first time I've seen her since the bumps first appeared. She still looks scared. I had called her as soon as I knew. She had seemed more fine with it at the time. Shock. It had to have been quite a shock. My crotch aches from the numerous burns, my genitals discolored by a patchwork of white marks around each bump. Her lips move and she repeats her mantra once again.

"I'm sorry. I just can't do this."

I don't have it in me to fight. It's only been a month and a half since we started. I have not let myself into it as I have in the past. I've not let myself fall head over heels like I have before. It makes it easier, simpler to emotionally walk away. I care for her, I enjoy her company, but I don't have it in me to fight for her. The lines that bind us are not that strong. My fears and worries have refused to let them strengthen too fast. I have not yet fully committed myself. I have not yet stopped considering alternatives. It's not hard to just let go.

"I understand."

We look at each other. Her hand falls away from mine. In silence she rises up from the couch and walks out the door. I hear the rattle of her car starting and then the sound of it driving away into the night. I sit on the couch by myself, numb and not feeling. A quiet voice in my head screams for her to come back. I can't blame her for her decision. If it was the other way around would I have done any different? Slowly I fall until I'm lying on my side. I feel empty. Just all so very empty. I lie there for half an hour, then rise, brush my teeth, and go to bed. A strand of her hair is on the pillow. I tell myself that I feel nothing when I take it to the bathroom to throw it away.

Attack

All of the muscles in my body are tense, ready to spring into action at a moment's notice. My shoulders rise higher than normal, an attempt to make myself look bigger, a leftover trait from our species' primal past. The energy courses through my body making the hair on the back of my neck and arms stand on end. My heart pounds in my chest. My breath, normal, feels rapid and uncontrolled. I'm on the edge and I am scared to death of falling off.

"Welcome to Subway, how may I help you sir?"

"A six inch meatball sub please."

I mumble my reply. My voice, normally booming and filled with confidence, is quiet in my own head. Barely perceptible to those around me.

"What was that sir?"

The worker behind the counter leans forward, hoping that the closer distance will aid him in hearing my stifled words.

"A six inch meatball sub on white please."

I say it a little louder. He seems to hear me this time, but my voice sounds far away in my own ears. I meet the eye of the man standing behind the counter, but only briefly. The eyes are the window to the soul. I don't want people looking into my soul right now. I don't want them to see the anxiety and the fear.

My foot begins to tap a quick rhythm as I watch my sandwich being made, a rapid percussive beat on the tile floor. My muscles will not loosen, if anything they tighten further. I will my foot to stop, my shoulders to lower, my body to relax. They obey me for a second, but as soon as my mind moves on to another thought, my shoulders begin to rise again. The fibers of muscles pull taut.

The making of the sandwich is a step by step process. Each step requires a question and an answer. With each answer I feel the need to look at the man behind the counter. I avoid looking him in the eye. I look at his nose, at his ear, at his mouth. Anything to avoid direct contact.

"Cheese?"

"Swiss."

"Toasted?"

"No."

"Toppings?"

"Black olives, mayonnaise, and red wine vinegar"

"Did you say pickles?"

"No."

Whenever I don't have to talk to him I look away. I look at the pictures of food on the wall above him. I look down at his hands preparing the sandwich as I give my directions. I look briefly at the other people in the store. Sometimes my eyes come to rest for brief moments, distracted, but only for a second. Sometimes I stare at those around me, the workers or my fellow customers, letting my eyes watch them at their work. The connection of watching someone is somehow soothing. When they feel me watching and look up, I quickly look away.

As I move forward along the sandwich assembly line I re-tuck my shirt for the fourth time since I've walked in. I'm hypersensitive. Every little piece that is out of place must be fixed. A nervous tick. A sign of someone having difficulty. I want to scream. I want to rip off my shirt and run around like an idiot. I feel like I'm about to explode. How can nobody notice this? They have to be able to notice. I can feel my skin literally buzzing with energy.

I reach forward to grab a bag of chips. I finger the packaging on the rack for a second before changing my mind and grabbing a different brand. I can feel people watching my every movement, feel them judging me. Look at that man. What the hell is wrong with him? He looks like a nervous wreck. Settle down fella. Just relax. What a basket case. I'm the only member of the audience for my little drama, but it feels as though all eyes are upon me.

The pace of my heart quickens. I reach up and clutch my chest for a moment like I'm having a heart attack. A silly notion. I'm as healthy as a horse. My mind and body are ready, waiting for the attack, waiting for the lion to leap out of the bushes to maul me. It's going to leap at any moment, my mind and body are convinced of it. Adrenaline courses through my veins in anticipation. I try to slow my breathing. I only have to survive this social savanna for a bit more.

I get to the register and open my wallet. My hands, normally steady and sure, are clumsy. I try to pull out seven dollars, two ones and a five, but it takes twice as long as normal. It's as though the hands picking through the wallet aren't mine. It's as though I'm controlling a robotic appendage from a distance away, watching via a camera with a long delay. Every command has to be several seconds ahead of the actual movement. I fumble through my wallet and pull out too much money. I use the back of my hand to press my wallet against my chest so I can use all of my fingers to clumsily separate out the extra bills.

The man behind the counter waits patiently. He's in no hurry. I feel like I'm being rushed. The lion is getting closer. I can sense him hiding somewhere nearby. He's crouching and ready to spring. I hand the money to the man and he hands me back my change. I grab my sandwich and shove the change in my pocket, a quarter escaping and falling onto the floor. I reach down quickly to grab it, my body shaking and my face red with embarrassment. My first attempt fails, as does my second. I can't get my fingernails under it. They are ragged and bitten. Please, come on, this is torment. The third attempt does the trick. I stand up and put the quarter in my pocket.

The man behind the counter smiles at me. I look back at the other waiting customers. Some faces are bored. Some are smiling at hidden thoughts. Some are mad and impatient at the added wait. Little worlds separated by space and the inability to communicate. I desperately want one to break through the divide. I desperately want to look one in the eye and feel a connection. I desperately want one to step forward to reassure me, tell me everything is going to be fine. All of the eyes are blank. All of the windows are opaque. I have to tell myself everything will be fine. My only advisor is someone I don't completely trust right now.

I walk hurriedly from the fast food eatery. My motions feel jerky and unnatural, as though my joints are held together by overly tightened rubber bands. Past the people eating at the tables, some alone and some with company. Some smiling and laughing. Some looking bored and weary. I can feel the hot breath of the lion on my neck. I can feel the wetness of my shirt at the small of my back and in my armpits. I escape out the door to safety. The lion falls behind. It's safer here. Safer outside. Here the private worlds around me are more spread out.

My furtive motions carry me back to my office. As I cross the bridge over the railroad tracks a quiet little voice tells me to jump over the railing. The logical part of my mind instantly pushes the thought back and for a second a very real fear of falling comes over me. It's an instant, just an instant. An instant where the tiny little voice had me convinced. I'm not suicidal, I don't want to die. I want to live. It's not a want to die that makes me think about jumping over the railing and falling the three stories to the railroad tracks below. It's only a desperate need to make something happen. It feels like something is going to happen. Waiting for something to happen is driving me insane. Maybe if something happens I won't feel like this anymore. Something. Anything.

I arrive at my building and get in the elevator with a woman who wears too much perfume. I want to yell at her to stop wearing so much perfume, that she has overdosed on her cure and it has become a poison. I worry that she can see the sheen of sweat across my brow, suspicious on a cold day. She gets off first, but her overpowering scent remains, a companion for the rest of my elevated journey. I breath through my mouth. I get off the elevator and the distraction is gone. My thoughts turn back to myself. A few more steps. Open and close the door. Make a friendly remark to the secretary. Walk into my office. Close the door behind me. Sit down in my chair.

I stare at the wall in front of me. My body is motionless, but my mind is an unstoppable machine of perpetual motion. It's just an anxiety attack. Just wait. It will pass. This isn't permanent. Just wait. Don't worry. Just breathe. My body and subconscious scream at me, calling the soothing voice a liar. You will always be this way. There is no escape. You are insane. You will never feel normal again. It's only a matter of time. I breathe deep and slow. In and out. I push the negative thoughts away. It's okay. Your body and brain are lying to you. They are just muscles having knee jerk reactions. These are battles you have fought before. You don't have to worry. You don't have to be scared. Just ride it out. You'll see.

I sit at my desk and shake, breathing deeply, repeating a soothing mantra in my head. This is not who I am, this is only temporary, this is not who I am, this is only temporary. I don't have to hide. I don't have to be afraid. The vibrations beneath my skin settle. My breath begins slowing and I feel some of the tension in my muscles ease. I'm not relaxed, but I'm at least looser. I have escaped again. I have made it through again. I unwrap my sandwich and open up a comedy website on my computer. I concentrate on the task at hand, one step at a time. The thoughts that set me off remain, but I ignore them, shoving them back where they are out of the way. It's over. It's passed. There's a voice in the back of my head that I do my best to ignore. For how long?

Mr. Campbell's Wild Ride

The Toyota Prius roars out of the parking garage of the resort hotel along Lake Coeur d'Alene. The sound of the engine, more the high pitched screaming of a cat than the low guttural roar of a lion, makes my heartbeat quicken. Movement to my left. I quickly apply the brakes and the car slows to a stop as the two oblivious figures, packed beneath their heavy winter finery, walk across the entrance to the garage. My fingers drum uselessly on the steering wheel as each footstep raises and drops in a slow plodding fashion that hints they are being affected by Einstein's theories of time dilation. My clock rushes forward at blistering speeds while theirs moves sloth like across the fourth dimension.

It is 6:08 PM. Forty miles separate me from my final goal of the Spokane Airport. Forty miles to cover before the deadline of 7:00 PM. Boarding time. Not making it is not an option. The two shiftless youths finally manage to drag themselves out of the beams of my headlights and I punch down on the accelerator. The gas engine of the hybrid kicks on and the front wheels spin ineffectively. Calming myself I let up, and push in the accelerator again with a more reasonable force. The car jerks forward and gains speed.

Turn out of the resort onto Second Street, hit a stoplight, wait, wait, wait. The light turns green, take a left onto Northwest Boulevard. Japanese restaurants, office buildings, the lake itself, all flit by in the flickering illumination of passing street lights. A thin layer of snow covers everything, turning the lake shore into a winter wonderland. I had walked along the lake earlier that day, the first time in years. My coat zipped up, my hat pulled low. Remembering times of my past. My hopes and dreams. My wishes for a better tomorrow. All the exact same today as when I had walked along that lake seven years before.

The last time I walked along the lake had been at a friend's wedding. I was just finishing up grad school. We had all ridden in a large boat from the resort to a nearby golf course. The reception had been amazing. Booze, dancing, friends. A sudden wind had come off the lake. The reception tent turned into a giant kite. People lifting me as we desperately tried to detach the canvas from the frame. One of the resort workers got tossed up into the air like a rag doll, desperately holding onto a rope like a demented Benjamin Franklin. Afterward it was back to the hotel, a random woman, a friend of the brides. We rode the elevator up and down, hid in little side hallways, and held closed doors to little rooms containing ice machines with our bodies. Kissing, licking, tugging, groping, caressing, exploring. I never talked to her again.

The snow does not matter. The roads are clear, dry, safe, no worries about black ice and the other varied dangers of winter driving. The winter is early, it's only mid-November. The weather has never asked for my opinion. One, two, three stoplights I luck out on, all green, all telling me to go, go, go. Evergreens, pine and fir, stand as tall sentinels along the street. They blend in with the cloudy darkening sky.

A long straight stretch, gas stations, warehouses, apartment buildings, used car lots. They all whip by. The car is going forty miles per hour, ten miles above the speed limit. My body jerks involuntarily. Pent up energy and tension releasing in one violent movement. I ignore it. It has nothing to do with me getting to my destination, so it's not important.

It was just a day meeting. Fly there in the morning, go to the meeting, fly back in the evening. A waste of my whole day to attend a three hour meeting. A three hour meeting I had to excuse myself out of early in order to head back to the airport. A waste of time, money, and energy. All just so my boss could say that someone from the company had been there. Just borrowing notes from one of the other attendees would have been just as effective.

They say that the majority of stop lights are timed so if you drive at a certain speed you will hit green lights the whole way down the street. Forty miles per hour is not this speed. I can see the countdown on the don't walk signs, a countdown to the yellow and then red which will slow my progress. I speed up and pass through one stoplight just as it turns yellow. I cross through a second intersection, the light turning red just as my rented car passes beneath it. The timing is off. I do not make the third light. This is the pattern for the next six lights. The acceleration from each green is quickly cut off by the next red. Stop and go. Stop and go.

I dislike board and committee meetings. The discussions are always the same. There is a problem. The problem needs to be addressed. First the problem must be described, most likely in an excruciatingly large amount of detail. Clarifications must be made, the problem must be restated in at least five different ways to make sure everyone understands it fully. If there is a problem there must obviously be a reason for the problem. Is the problem the fault of the person who brought up the problem? Is the only reason the problem exists because that person wasn't up to doing whatever task revealed the problem? Discussion. No, the problem is an actual problem for everyone. Is there anyone else that can be blamed for the problem? Discussion. Maybe it's the.....? No, no, let's move forward, not look back. Are there any solutions to the problem? Discussion. Ideas. Everyone talking about and debating their ideas. Nobody listening well enough to realize they're actually debating for the same solution. Do we have an idea? Good, good, let's table this item until the next meeting to give us all time to think about it.

This process takes up the vast majority of the meeting. I can see a solution to the problem within five minutes. I'm sure others can too. But protocols must be followed. No one sticks their neck out without feeling that the whole group will go along with them. It does not matter that I see a solution. I've been ordered to keep my trap shut. I am only an observer, a watcher, a spectator, not part of the action. I do not feel bad that I have to leave early. I've already seen this episode. I already have a pretty good idea how it will turn out. Life has always been this way. Knowing what needs to be done but never being able to do it.

The left turn light changes to green and I swing the car around onto the on-ramp. The accelerator goes to the floor and the car rushes forward. Thirty, forty, fifty, sixty, seventy miles per hour. Interstate 90, a slab of concrete and asphalt that stretches over three thousand miles from Seattle to Boston. I'm

216

only going to need a little piece of it. The clock on the dashboard says 6:18 PM. I still have thirty-seven miles to go. I turn on the radio and search the airwaves until a station blares to life with the sounds of eighties hair bands. This is the kind of situation that this music was written for.

The miles blur behind me. The car speeds effortlessly forward. I've traveled this highway before, though it has been a while. College days, driving to Montana to stay at a hot springs, everyone drunk but the driver. A heavy snowstorm had made the trip slow. So did stopping every thirty miles so someone could get out and pee. We were never welcome at that resort again. My memory is a little fuzzy. I believe we were finally kicked out after two days for disturbing the other guests. One friend wore a beer box on his head the whole time to protect his noggin after nearly knocking himself out on a ceiling fan the first night. In a later rematch it proved ineffectual. The whole time I felt slightly separate and awkward. I was just out of high school. The sign welcoming people to the hot springs mysteriously disappeared. I had no part in it.

Welcome to Post Falls. Only thirty miles to go. It's 6:25 PM. I'm making good time. Traffic starts to get heavier, more people clogging my straight shot. It's the rule of the world, if you have to go somewhere in a hurry, some asshole will be driving slow in the left lane of the freeway. My bane is an old beige Oldsmobile, driving at an even pace with the car next to it in the right lane. No way to get around, no way to get past.

"Fuck you, you god damn cock sucking piece of shit!"

My cries of rage boom across the car's interior, but are ineffectual, only I can hear them. The jackass is holding me back. Slowing from seventy-five to fifty-five makes the car feel like it's going at a snail's pace. I swear I can see the digital lights of the clock begin to move upward more swiftly. My hands pound on the steering wheel as more curses escape my lips. I get right on the asshole's back end, tailgating in hopes he'll get the idea and either speed up or get out to the way. My attempts to influence him prove just as ineffectual as my cries of rage.

We cross the Idaho-Washington border, twenty-five miles to go, 6:30 PM. The crossing is smooth. I remember when I was a kid we drove across and there was a definite bump as the freeway condition suddenly got different in Idaho. It's no longer obvious. Does that mean things are better in Idaho now or worst in Washington? The Oldsmobile, without signaling, speeds up and moves into the right lane, then takes the exit toward Stateline strip club. Thank god. The driver is a pervert. The Prius revs its engine and the speedometer climbs back up to seventy-five.

Breakups are never easy, especially when it becomes obvious one party felt something more than the other did. I had been just about to go to bed when the phone rang.

"Rob's girlfriend broke up with him." My answer is a grunt. "We're getting him drunk. He wants to go to Stateline. You in?"

"Let me put on some pants."

It takes two hours to drive from Moscow to Spokane. Two hours is plenty of time to get drunk enough to convince yourself it's a good idea. On the plus side Rob had been a fairly cheerful drunk, not a sad mopey drunk who only wanted to talk about his ex. Stateline was not a classy place, but it was the only strip club nearby. Rob and the others were enamored, I was not. I do not know why I went. Strippers always make me feel sad. Nobody starts out life hoping to be a stripper, and most definitely not a stripper at Stateline. There was a man and his wife my parents' age on the other side of the stage. He made his wife hold his hat when the stripper let him motorboat her. The wife did not look happy. We left soon after. Rob was a mopey drunk on the ride home. I couldn't help, his problem wasn't something I understood.

Liberty Lake, Greenacres, Spokane Valley. The towns pass by one by one. Twenty-two miles, twenty miles, sixteen miles to go. I have to slow every now and again as cars enter the left lane to avoid trucks, but the slow ones return to the right once they have passed. The faster ones get in a line behind the blazing comet that is the bright red rented Toyota Prius controlled by slight shifts of my hands and feet. The clock ticks upward, but its pace feels slowed. I'm outrunning everything, even time itself. There is no stopping me.

Giggles was from this area, another small town on a lake, a description that matches the majority of the towns in the vicinity. Giggles, the girl who called me her cabana boy, the one who had laughed so hard at the ridiculousness of it all when we first made out that she forever earned a nickname. She was strange, sometimes cold, sometimes hot, never in between. Something had been wrong. Some kind of anxiety that could not be shared. Looking back now it seems fairly obvious, but at the time I just didn't know.

I was a late bloomer, having no idea, trying to act like I did. I don't think she knew any more than me. Months of hot and cold coming to a head one night with a bottle of wine. Kissing, caressing, the feel of wanting someone who wants you. The feel of her small tits in my hand, her small erect nipples between my fingers. She got up from the couch, lit some candles, turned off the lights. Things continued and she took me in her mouth. She was one of my best friends. The elation, the sensation, the culmination, things you do not forget. When it was finished I was scared and confused, I did not know what to do. The look on her face as she looked back at me mirrored my own. I got up and left her apartment without a word. I was just some scared guy who had no idea what he was doing. No clue what to say or do. Just overwhelmed. It's been seven years since that night, and I am still that person.

The car keeps going between sixty-five and seventy-five. I'm trying to keep it below seventy but the energy flowing through my body keeps forcing the needle up higher. The car ahead, is that what I think it is? Are those lights or is it just a luggage rack? Fuck. I slow the car down, faster than I should. Shit, it is a cop car. I pull up alongside, my speed reduced to fifty-five. It's too late, the cop car slows and turns into my lane, red and blue lights begin to flash. I pull across the lanes of traffic and stop on the side of the road, the police car following. My headlong flight has been halted. I am twelve miles short of my escape from this place. It's 6:40 PM.

I've heard before that all cops are either the kids who were bullies in school or the kids that got bullied. I don't know if this is true. What I do know is that they are in a position of power and they know it. Some people yell and rail against the police, others lie and make up stories. I've always found it easier to be polite and honest. I do my best, but I can feel the seconds trickle by as the officer goes through the slow monotony that every driver knows by heart.

"Please turn off the radio. License. Registration. Do you know how fast you were going? Do you know what the speed limit is here? Why were you in such a hurry? I'll be right back."

My fingers drum the steering wheel with nervous energy. I was so close. So very close. The man sitting in the car is no different than the man who traveled these roads seven years ago. The setting and actors may have changed, but the play's plot has remained the same. All I wanted was to get home. All I have ever wanted is to get home. The clock and the police officer do not care. 6:43, 6:45, 6:47. I resign myself to my fate. I'll never be able to make the flight. There is not another one until tomorrow. I will have to stay the night. The police officer gives me a ticket for $144 and sends me on my way. It's 6:50 PM.

I drive the speed limit of sixty miles per hour. I don't want to get pulled over a second time. I feel beaten, defeated, my goals unobtained. My heart no longer races with adrenaline. My body no longer quivers. I have been subdued. Just another bad hand dealt in the grand game of life. My brain begins to formulate plans on what to do. Return the rental car, see about changing my ticket over to tomorrow, get a room at one of the nearby hotels. My brain is good at quickly adapting to the situations it finds itself in. It's had a lot of practice. Things are going to be okay, they didn't turn out the way I wanted them to, but they are going to be okay. I turn off the freeway at the exit to the airport, four miles to go, it's 6:58.

My foot ignores the orders from my brain and begins pressing downwards on the accelerator. My rented car begins to gain speed. I'm so close. I'm not yet beaten. Not this time. I don't want to stay the night in Spokane. I want to go home. I feel my energy return. It's not over yet. The last four miles disappear and I pull into the rental car parking area. I leave the car alongside the curb still running, yelling at a surprised attendant that I have a flight to catch. It's 7:03.

Spokane airport is not large, but it's long, just one long continuous hallway with my gate at the opposite end from the rental car desk. I run. I run like an Olympic athlete looking to beat every record in the book. The airport is quiet, all the shops closed up, mine is the last flight of the night. My polo shirt begins to soak through with sweat, my heavy winter coat is on, still zipped up. My legs pound, eating the distance. With a rush I'm at the security point, the only one at the checkpoint, everyone else has already gone through. Take off my shoes. Take off my coat. Take off my hat. Take off my belt. All go into the gray security baskets. All go through the x-ray machine. It's 7:09.

Before me is the last great obstacle, the metal detector. The TSA agent waves me forward and I close my eyes and pray as I slowly step through it. The machine stands, silently, I have passed through the gate. My belongings come out of the x-ray

221

machine, nothing suspicious about any of them. I don't bother putting back on my shoes and belt. I grab everything under my arm and start running again, running as fast as I can. I see the airline workers starting to close the door....so close.

"Wait!!!"

They startle easily. They stare at my running form and I can see the thoughts behind their eyes, the gears of decision cranking away with no sign of whether it will be a positive or negative outcome. Everything seems to slow down, and just as I lose hope the eyes relent and the door is pulled back open. I've made it. I have to paw through my pocket to find my ticket. Shit, where is it? Here it is. They scan it and send me through. I walk down the tunnel and onto the plane, my head held high, my shoes, belt, coat, and hat under my arm. The others passengers gawk as I take my seat, a satisfied smile on my face. Today I triumphed.

An Unwanted Gift
Part 3

"Not in front of my cart! Not in front of my cart!!"

The cries of the owner of the food cart register in my ears, but it's far too late to stop the boiling over torrent from pouring out of my mouth. My body bends over and heaves, ejecting corned beef and cabbage, four pickled eggs, and twelve, or possibly more, Guinness's onto the sidewalk in front of me. My friends and other random Saint Paddy's Day revelers laugh and snap pictures of my shame and discomfort. I can't blame them. It's not every day you see an extremely drunk man in a fashionable green dress puking out his guts so hard it brings tears to his eyes. Either way, I'm in no condition to chastise anyone for their lack of sympathy.

I spit to clear my mouth of the horrible taste, wishing I could clear my head as easily. The world spins around me in a frightful dance that threatens to bring up what little remains in my stomach. The commuter train pulls into the nearby station and my friends half carry and half drag me into it, throwing me unceremoniously into an empty seat. I mumble incoherently and spit uncouthly on the floor, still trying to clear my mouth of the taste of bile. My head overflows with anger and frustration. Him. She has gone home with him. Just the sudden change in attitude was bad enough, but to have someone like him benefit from it is almost too much to bear.

It's a shock to the system. Something has changed so quickly that I find myself reeling to keep up. Just the night before we had been cuddled together in a bed, talking through the night. Today she is distant and far away, flirting with every man she can and dancing with the bastard, a man who epitomizes sleaze and self-centeredness. I try to dance with her myself, but she only gets mad. The distance which I had been unable to force myself to bridge was now biting me in the ass.

I want what I can't have. My mind and body are betraying me. The day was already being taken up by drinking, of course it was only natural to continue that trend, just at an increased level. Anger, frustration, and jealousy. All of it roils together in my head and gut. I feel sick inside. I have no idea what to do. Lacking in options I pour Guinness after Guinness down my throat. Friends come and talk to me and I loudly bellow out my frustrations, asking for questions and advice, none of which are usable in my steadily strengthening inebriation.

Drunkenly slurring I try to talk to her once again, but her friends block me. She gets upset, but says nothing. She grabs her coat and bag and leaves to go to the after party at his house. The bastard. The rotten bastard. My friends sit me down and give me another beer. My anger and frustration overflow and I pound my fist down on the table, upending glasses which my friends frantically grab before they roll onto the floor. The bartender is giving me sideways glances, but I don't care. Fucking bastard.

My friends hoist me up. I resist at first, but they tell me they're taking me to the after party, so I change my attitude. I get up and walk unsteadily out of the bar. My friends take me to a different bar where they attempt to distract me and resolutely refuse to talk about the things which are currently upsetting me so much. It's a good call on their part. Even I can see that. It's why I consider them friends. I play along. I do my best to act light hearted and talk about nicer things. However, the problem still gnaws at my middle. My attempts to drown it with beer only meet with disastrous results, both for me and the owner of the food cart.

We lie on the fold out couch together, lightly clasping each other, lying face to face. We ask each other questions. We chip away at the walls between us, getting to know one another. I tell her more than I've told anyone in a long time. Some of the things I tell her I've never told anyone else. It feels good to let the words flow. My psyche is covered in scars, disasters of past relationships, things that are hard to explain, and portions which I feel I can't describe. She's the first to ask questions. She's the first to enquire about the clues which bubble to the surface. She's one of the first people in a long time that I want to talk to about it. I struggle with it. I don't know how to explain. Much of it is still so fresh and painful though so much time has passed. More than a year. It doesn't matter. It still feels as fresh as the day before. I struggle with it. I don't know how to explain it. It doesn't matter. It's not the most immediate problem.

She says things as well. Private things. Secret things. I hold her close and give her hand a squeeze whenever I feel it's appropriate. A reminder that somebody else is here. I want to kiss her, but I dare not. It's starting to get strange that I haven't tried to kiss her. Neither of us has said anything, but I can feel it. I worry if I don't do something she'll start to think that I'm not interested in her. What else is she supposed to think? She's giving me the look, but I do nothing. I don't know how to bring it up. I can't get myself to say anything. I can't get myself to risk the rejection. Memories of so many rejections are still fresh in my mind, but one in particular stands out. The most recent one. I don't say anything. Instead I just lay stewing in my own frustrations, watching my chances wither on the vine.

Just a few days before I had received my third treatment for molluscum. The third time of laying on a paper covered examination table. The third time of the doctor burning the newly appeared bumps with liquid nitrogen. I'm getting frustrated. Three times. Three times I've been told that this treatment will take care of the problem. Three times of subjecting myself to pain, anguish, and embarrassment. Three fucking times. Each one followed by a rising hope and elation overpowering the sting, only to be dashed by the reappearance of bumps within a week. This time is no different. A few small ones had appeared on my shaft just the day before I found myself in this bed.

There are so many things that I want, but I don't dare do anything. Yes, it would just be a kiss, but what if it progressed further? How could I tell her so that she just wouldn't disappear in disgust and horror, just as with the one before? I don't know what to do, so I do nothing. I lay there next to her, lightly stroking her hand, the two of us talking into the night.

She stands perfectly still. The calf watches her intently and takes a nervous step forward, its curiosity overcoming its fear. The calf's mother stands nearby, contentedly eating hay with her fellows, hay that we have only recently just thrown from the back of the pickup as it slowly ground its way forward in first gear. The calf takes another wary step forward and I smile to myself as I see her hold her breath. She leans forward slowly, hopefully, and extends a hand for the calf to sniff. The calf looks at her hand and then back at its mother. It takes one more step forward, and then turns and bolts down the hill. She looks back at me with a disappointed smile on her face.

Snow covered hills surround the valley of my childhood home. My sanctuary. My safe haven. The place that no matter where I go, will always be home. She's the first woman I've ever brought here. I'm glad I've brought her. We both needed an adventure. I had told her about my home. The secluded world where I grew up. I had told her about feeding the cows hay, the calves being born, and the masses of curious babes running across the bunchgrass covered hillsides. She had wanted to see it, so I brought her.

As we walk back to the pickup I try to hide my discomfort. The molluscum itch and rub uncomfortably against the tight cotton fabric of my long johns. The second treatment has failed, just as the first before it. The molluscum have come back. The third treatment is scheduled for Monday. The doctor has assured me that this one will likely do the trick. In some ways I'm glad for the molluscum. Their presence removes sex as an option. It has allowed me to get to know Adeline better than I might have otherwise. My dad starts the pickup. She thinks he looks like Clint Eastwood. I don't see it, but who am I to argue? We get in. My dad puts it in gear and the pickup makes its way toward the gate leading out of the pasture.

We sit and talk over drinks, but I have to leave soon. I'm supposed to meet Katy for dinner. I'm worried about it. This is the first time I've seen her since I told her about my molluscum contagiosum. We're all packed together in the booth. I've enjoyed the company of the woman sitting next me. Her name is Adeline. I like listening to her talk and telling jokes to make her laugh. She has a nice laugh. I enjoy saying things that shock or appall her a little bit. She seems to enjoy my company just as much as I enjoy hers.

Who knows how these things get started. I don't really understand the laws of attraction. I've never been able to describe what attributes create that spark. It's a combination of so many different things coming together. Every mix is unique, but everyone has things that are similar. I've certainly never been able to identify what attracts women to me, but there must be something because it happens from time to time. Why wonder about it? Especially given the existence of another. The only division between them is time, it's not a matter of one being better than the other. Like so many things in life, it comes down to seniority.

I check my watch again, put some money on the table to pay for my drinks, and then signal for others to rise to let me escape from the confines of the booth. It's time for me to go. I say my goodbyes and head for the door. I look back at her before heading out into the cold. She's listening to someone else, but glances over to watch me for just a moment. There's definitely something there. A potential that will be left unexplored. I'm attracted to her, there's no denying it, but that doesn't mean I have to do anything about it.

My friends drag me off the commuter train and down the street. They're going to another bar, but I will not be joining them. A small group of volunteers take me into the basement of a nearby house and dump me onto a couch. One, a wife of another, pulls my shoes off my feet and covers me with a blanket so I'll stay warm. It's too cold to leave me with just the questionable coverage provided by my green dress. I try to babble incoherently of the injustices of the world, but getting nowhere, shift to drunkenly apologizing for my condition. My friend looks down at me and frowns.

"There are so many good things about you, but you need to get your shit together."

She turns and walks up the stairs, turning off the light as she goes. I wallow in the darkness. Clinging to the words.

Time's Pace

Sometimes I feel like I'm traveling through time faster than everybody else. It's a weird feeling to have. My days tend to be packed full. Toil away on three or four different projects at work, meet a friend for lunch, get out of work and go for a run, go drinking afterwards with friends, go home, watch some television, go to bed. I don't really think I'm any busier than anyone else per se. I know lots of people who describe their days in ways that make them sound twice as busy.

It's not something I notice while I'm actually going through the motions. When I'm interacting with others I don't see them moving in slow motion or anything like that. Though at times I do feel like my mind is working faster, always two steps ahead of the conversation, though to be fair it depends on the person. I definitely feel like my mind moves faster than my physical body is able to keep up with. My brain is constantly boiling over with thoughts, dreams, ideas, ruminations, and practiced conversations. My mind often travels faster than my mouth. It makes it difficult to express myself. Though I imagine this is not a unique characteristic.

No, it's not something I notice in the moment. Rather it's something I notice when the day is done and I try to think back on it. When I think back over my day it is as though the concept of time has been skewed. What was only a few hours ago feels as though it happened a day ago. What happened the day before feels like it happened a week ago. What happened a week ago feels like a month ago. What happened a month ago feels like a year ago. It's a strange sensation.

My days are completely filled with so many varied activities, each one requiring me to be a different person. The man I am at work is not the man I am amongst friends, the man I am with my family, the man I am when I'm by myself. It's like I'm living numerous lives all at the same time. Switching from one to the other as needed. Each with its individual wants, needs, demands, and social circles. Perhaps it's the wide variety of thoughts this creates that is the problem. Constantly jumping from one to another depending on whom I'm interacting with or what I'm thinking about at any given moment. I don't imagine this is very unique either. I imagine lots of people find themselves living multiple lives at the same time, each with its own societal constraints.

Perhaps the problem is not that I'm moving faster through time, but maybe it's the fact that all the memories seem so similar that my mind can no longer discern the difference between a memory from last month and a memory from three years ago. Time continues to move forward, but the story doesn't change. Don't get me wrong. The world does change.

The characters change. The plot changes. The scenery changes. Comedy and tragedy, new problems and opportunities arise. The issue is that through it all the basic theme of the story remains unchanged. I am a rock in a river. The river shifts its depth and courses around me, but I remain in the same place. Deep inside I am still a scared child, desperately wanting to make a connection, desperately wanting somebody to understand.

A Strange Morning

All in all it wasn't a bad apartment. Two bedrooms, one bath, all the appliances provided, and reasonable rent for the area. Not too bad of a deal at all. About the only complaint I had was the neighbor. Out the backdoor was a balcony and a staircase that led down to the ground three stories below. For some reason on the landing just below mine there was a small nook of an apartment. I don't really know if it was truly small, but the door was much smaller than all the other doors. For all I knew Times Square could be behind that door. It was strange, just being on that landing between floors, sitting by itself.

Within that apartment lived the biggest man I had ever seen. He looked like a shaved Clydesdale. I called him Alepati.

I highly doubt that was his real name, but I didn't know his actual one. He didn't speak a word of English, but instead communicated in what sounded like a person talking while keeping their tongue on the roof of their mouth. From his appearance I guessed he was some kind of Pacific islander, probably from Guam or Samoa, but since I had no idea what you call someone from Guam I just assumed he was Samoan. He usually kept to himself, but always played techno music very loudly at all hours of the day. Sometimes he would randomly stick his head out his door when I was on the balcony and yell something in Samoan at me. I knew it couldn't be polite because even though he didn't speak English he had clearly gotten the gist of our hand gestures.

So, aside from one crazy Pacific islander it was probably the most perfect apartment I had ever lived in. By far the best feature was the fact that it was only a few blocks away from Moscow's Main Street and the bars that were on it, an important factor for any college kid. This is where the story really begins, the morning after a hard night of boozing and sad attempts to get laid.

I woke up and rolled over onto the cold side of my bed. This spot was always cold, the much needed soft female body meant to warm it up always missing. However, I wasn't too discouraged this morning by the lack of female company. Any man who drunkenly attempts to take home the largest woman in the bar is little disappointed to find himself alone in the morning. Sunlight brightened the entire room and from the clock on my desk it was apparent that most of the morning had already gone by. I would have just rolled over and gone back to sleep, but the pressure building in my bladder forced me to take other actions.

Since I was up I decided might as well face the day. After cleaning the last clinging pieces of vomit from the toilet bowl with nature's disinfectant, I took a shower to wash away the stink of cigarettes, stale booze, and whatever rank perfume Ms.

Piggy from last night had been wearing. Having gone through my morning rituals I went to the kitchen to try and replace the dinner I had lost the night before. It was while chugging from the jug of slightly sour milk that I first noticed something amiss in my fridge. A large bite had been taken out of the middle of the block of cheese. Grains of Copenhagen were slathered around the teeth marks. It could only mean one thing. Dusty had been here.

Dusty not only had been here, he still was here. I found him sleeping in my chair in the living room, chew spit seeping from the corners of his mouth, glasses crooked on his face, pants unzipped, clutching himself. I never really understood people's need to hold themselves. Perhaps he was afraid that his dick would take the opportunity provided by his slumber to pack up its balls and leave. Regardless I didn't try to wake him since he seemed to be pretty well passed out. However, still a little silly from the booze I did make full use of his comatose state to draw a large handlebar mustache on his face using a black permanent marker.

Having fully entertained myself at Dusty's expense, I sat on the couch and turned on the television, catching *Smokey and the Bandit* pretty close to the beginning of the movie. Turning up the volume so I could hear over the beeps and boops emanating from Alepati's hole in wall, I settled down to wait for Dusty to return to the world of the living and explain what the hell he was doing in my apartment on a Sunday morning.

Dusty didn't wake up till the movie was over and I'd watched most of a *Dukes of Hazzard* episode. You know the one, where the Dukes defeat Boss Hogg's latest get rich quick scheme. Anyway, I was quite surprised when I heard him speak.

"I need to borrow your car for awhile."

I was a bit confused by his statement, which should have really been more of a question. Few people ever wanted to borrow my car. It was a '93 Ford Tempo with moderate body damage, a car so shoddy people who drove Yugos made fun of you for owning one. I usually left the keys in it figuring anyone stealing it was probably in a lot worse shape than I was.

"What do you need my car for?"

"I got a new job working for Wal-Mart in Winchester, your car gets better mileage than my pickup."

Again stunned silence from me. His story made little sense at all. Winchester was a little town that sat on Highway 95, the only connecting route between northern and southern Idaho. It only had about five hundred people in it and was two hours south of Moscow. Questions filled my head. Since when was there a Wal-Mart in Winchester? Better yet, why would Dusty drive two hours south to work a minimum wage job? Even better yet, why would Wal-Mart hire Dusty?

Alepati's techno music emanating from the wall filled the silence. Mistaking my stupid blank look for one of refusal Dusty was quick to try and seal the deal.

"I'll pay for the gas and give you a little extra for wear and tear?"

"How much?"

"Ten bucks a day."

This was a strangely generous offer. Maybe Dusty had something going on with an old logger wife or something. Whatever it was, the Tempo had never seemed so valuable. However, it was at that moment that I first noticed the strange swelling in Dusty's face. It looked horrible. His skin was turning a strange color of purple and his face was getting all puffy, especially around the eyes.

"What's wrong with your face?"

"What in the hell are you talking about? Will you quit stalling and give me a damn answer?"

I decided that if Dusty didn't notice the swelling it was probably best to take a spectator's position on the situation. I again mulled over the Tempo question, watching his steadily swelling face with a keen scientific interest. Perhaps it was some kind of allergic reaction to the cheese or permanent marker. They were both of the cheaper varieties. I had to stay focused. One problem still nagged me about the car.

"What am I going to drive while you got my car?"

"You can use my pickup."

"Okay, let me get the keys."

"Already have them."

"Oh," I paused to consider if this should upset me and decided not to care. After all, it was Dusty. "I guess I'll see you later then."

"See you later."

With that Dusty got up, zipped up his pants, and headed out the sliding glass back door, still oblivious to his swelling face which had started to push the glasses off of his nose. I was so enthralled with this strange phenomenon that I didn't even think of the fact that he hadn't given me the keys to his pickup, or that it was early afternoon and I still hadn't put on any pants. What I did notice though was the large rat that slipped in through the glass door just as Dusty closed it.

It was obvious that this was no ordinary rat. For one thing it looked fat and well fed. For another it was completely shaved. It sat next to the door twitching its nose and studying me. I should probably mention that I hate rats. Mice are all right, but rats just give me the chills. The fact that I wasn't wearing pants only added to my disgust. Something had to be done. With a blood curdling scream I lifted the easy chair that Dusty had recently vacated, ran over, and smashed it down upon the rat. It let out a squeal that would put any pig to shame, and then was quiet.

For the first time since I had moved in Alepati's techno music stopped playing. I heard his door fly open and his heavy feet running up the stairs, then a boom as his heavy body burst through my glass door, the glass cracking with the force of

Alepati forcing. Flinging aside my chair he looked down at the crushed body of the rat. Alepati's wide face became dark with sadness and rage. Tears streamed from his eyes. I could not understand a word of the screams in his native tongue that he threw upon me, but I quickly came under the impression that I had not only killed the big Samoan's pet, but also his most precious friend.

I was desperately trying to get my hungover brain to think of a way out of this mess when Alepati scooped me up like a rag doll, carried me outside, lifted me over his head, and threw me from the third floor balcony. As I fell all I could think was how I wished I had put on some pants.

It was at this moment that I awoke in my bed covered in sweat. I rolled over onto the cool side of the bed, the side that I felt lucky didn't contain the woman I had been hitting on the night before. It had all seemed so strange, but yet so real. I cowered under my blankets, afraid to emerge into the possibly preordained future. My body and mind refused to let go of the feeling of falling. When the pressure in my bladder became too much, I chose to wet the bed instead of facing the possibility. It was only afterwards that I remembered there was no Samoan, but it was a little too late to feel relieved.

An Unwanted Gift Part 4

The April rains lash against the window, creating a percussion that rises and falls with the tempo of the wind. I lay in a sodden heap on the futon, covered with a single blanket. My body feels strung out, beaten, trodden on. Six hours hotboxing cigars in a tool shed will do that to you. So will two thirds of a bottle of Jameson combined with an especially bad McDonald's cheeseburger. All have taken their toll. All have worked together to sap my strength and force the evacuation of fluids from both ends of my body. I lay, unable to sleep, fearing a racking cough that will restart the flows that I have only managed to barely get under control.

I hear her moan in the room next to mine. It rises and falls, punctuating the rustling of two bodies moving frantically against each other. The unmistakable wet sweaty sounds of two people, if not having sex, doing everything up to it. I plug my ears and try to ignore it. I pray for a harsher storm. One which would bring fear even to Noah. Anything to drown out the sounds emanating through the wall. It's unfair. It's not right. I have to accept the world as it is, but must I be tormented by it? I had been looking forward to this night. I had been looking forward to the escape. An activity where there would be no chance of running into her. Now I'm trapped. Unable to leave. Unable to fall asleep. Unable to block the sounds I don't want to hear. I'm in hell.

The telltale bumps returned the night before, marking the failure of the fourth treatment. My doctor had grown tired of treating me, exasperated with seeing her attempts fail again and again. Admitting defeat she had sent me to a specialist, a dermatologist. My spirits had been low, but the idea of a specialist had brought new hopes. Wasted hopes. A nicer waiting room, a better examination room, a higher cost to my insurance, but the exact same treatment method. Liquid nitrogen to my genitals has become commonplace. I barely even shed a tear. There's nothing to be done. This is my life now and I must learn to accept it.

A guy's poker night should be a safe place. A place where I don't have to watch the budding romance between her and one of my friends. At the very least he isn't the bastard. He's a nice guy. So I guess that's something. To be honest, I would be hard pressed to say a single negative thing about him. However, he could be the nicest man in the world, but it doesn't mean I want a front row seat to their courtship. One moment a group of us are playing poker, the next they all show up drunk. A collection of inebriates led by the host's wife. Debaucherous revelers howling their delight into the night. Her friends are my friends. There is no escape.

They crowd into the toolshed, filling every nook and cranny. She draws up next to me, emerging from the cigar smoke and imperiously demanding a drink of some of my whiskey. What can I do? I don't want to give it to her, but I give it to her anyway. I can see him in the background. Smiling and laughing, casting the occasional hungry glance in her direction. The poker game falls apart, giving way to a party which moves into the house. I don't know what else to do, so I escape into the bottle. Golden liquid please set me free from my madness. I escape out onto the porch. She finds me there. She needs to talk to somebody. She has worries. We all have fucking worries.

Why does it have to be me? I don't want to hear about her problems. It's not that I wish her any ill, or that I don't care what happens to her, I just don't want to play emotional support for a woman who has rejected me. I'm a man damn it. A fucking man. Not one of her girlfriends. Why can't she talk to him? Why does she have to talk to me? I say nothing. I listen and provide comfort. I'm not a man. I'm a eunuch. The molluscum has castrated me as surely as a knife.

She goes on and on and I listen. I nod and try to be a good friend. That's what you're supposed to do. You're supposed to be a good friend. You're supposed to do the right thing. Maybe I can tell her my own problem, but what would be the point? It's too late now. The time has passed. The world has moved on, leaving me behind. She hugs me and I hug her back. I can feel them down there. The source of my damnation. What does it matter anymore? It's my problem. Not hers. I've been silent past the point of there being any reason to speak. She breaks away and goes back inside. I sit out in the cold with my whiskey and brood. A few drops of rain fall from the sky. Harbingers of what is to come. I can see them through the glass. They're talking and laughing, all worries forgotten. My stomach tightens into a knot, gurgles, and loosens again.

I stay on the porch until the rain and my gut forces me to go inside. There are fewer people now. They have begun to scatter, but the two I wish would leave are sitting on the couch. I'm far too drunk to drive. Between bouts in the bathroom I gain the host's permission to sleep in one of their two extra rooms. I retreat again to do battle, but find myself overwhelmed by the vileness of my insides performing a flanking maneuver through my mouth. I collapse onto the bathroom mat, my eyes filled with tears of frustration at my devastation. When I emerge the house is dark and nobody is there. I go into the room designated by my host, take off my shoes, and pull myself weakly onto the futon.

Each moan echoes through my head, ricocheting from ear to ear, a hellish cacophony. I can't take it. I can't take it anymore. How long can such things last? How much must I endure in silence? I shakily rise up from the futon where I lay. I push one foot ahead of the next. My fist rises into the air and falls. Three sharp knocks sound on the dividing wall. All sounds cease but the falling rain. I climb back onto the futon, hoping desperately for sleep to overtake me before the sounds of pleasure renew.

Viewpoints

Trevor

He slid it in. She gave out a stifled moan. Trevor smiled to himself. It was unbelievable, unfathomable, unexpected. Here he was, Trevor Johnson, living a fantasy straight out of one of the porno videos he so often sweatily clicked on with shaking hands each night before he went to bed. He thrust himself into the woman. Her round shapely ass pressed back against him, his hands tightly holding her hips. He looked across her back, covered by her still buttoned blouse, to the blonde covered head laying on her crossed arms on the back of the toilet. He wondered if he should grab her hair and give it a tug like the men in the videos did. He began to move his hand, but lost confidence before it even got to her back. The hip seemed the safer choice.

Trevor had been drinking a beer alone at the bar. He was not a big drinker, and rarely ever stopped for libations after work, though he had driven by the bar a thousand times on his way home. But that night the idea of going straight home filled him with disgust. Another day, just another day of failing because he couldn't get up the guts to open his mouth. So many things that he wanted. A raise, more respect, a date with the cute girl at the supermarket, but he just couldn't get himself to ask. He'd been mulling his lack of loquaciousness when she had sat down.

He hadn't even noticed her walk in. An older woman, probably in her late forties, but still good looking. It was obvious that she worked hard to keep herself an attractive. She had been dressed like a real estate agent. Knee high skirt, sky blue blouse, several bracelets on one arm, and a wedding ring prominently on her finger. She had sat down and ordered a beer, looking every bit as dejected with life as he did.

The woman continued to breath heavily in time with Trevor's thrusts as he quickened his pace in excitement. How in the hell had he ended up in this glorious position, taking a woman from behind in a dive bar bathroom? Maybe his self-loathing had finally hit its breaking point? Maybe it was the three beers already in him? Whatever the reason, Trevor had surprised himself when he had offered to buy the woman a drink. Next thing he knew they were sitting next to each other and talking. He wasn't Trevor. He was witty, urbane, and charming. She laughed at his jokes, smiled at his stories, and blushed at his compliments. He was everything that he had ever wanted to be. Everything that he really wasn't.

Trevor's breathing got harder. He had never felt so alive. Never felt so sexually excited. Never felt so in control. The stars had aligned. A few drinks. Casual talk turning into alluring glances. An accidental brushing of one's legs ending with the two limbs pressed together. A soft touch to an arm or hand to make a point. The bartender had gone into the backroom. She had stood and grabbed his hand. Before Trevor could say anything she had dragged him back into the men's room.

Trevor's confusion had been quickly replaced by a flurry of lips and limbs as she pulled him into the nearest stall. She had held him tightly, tongues entwined, his hands groping and squeezing her body as she unzipped his pants and rubbed his shaft. Trevor was in new waters, but he had gladly let himself get swept away into the current of alcohol and hormones. He had reached to unbutton her blouse, but she had grabbed his hands and pulled them down, guiding them under her skirt to the warmth between her legs. The woman had moaned and quivered with his touch. She had pulled down her underwear and lifted up her skirt. Then she turned around and bent herself over the toilet.

"Fuck me, god fuck me now," she had rasped. Trevor had obliged.

Trevor could feel the woman tighten down upon him. He could hold it in no longer. With a shudder and a moan he ejected himself into her, squeezing her hips so hard he left bruises. The woman pushed him backward out of her, stood up, pulled her skirt down, and turned around. For a moment she stared at him blankly, and then she brushed past him out of the stall. Trevor turned to watch her go and sat wearily on the toilet seat, sweating, gasping, smiling. He heard the bathroom door open and close. He saw her underwear lying on the ground where she had left it. None of it registered in his mind. All he could feel was elation. A single thought echoed through his mind. I can do anything. I can do anything. I can do anything.

Rita

He slid it in. She started to moan, but bit her lip to stifle it. He thrust himself into her wetness and Rita, her head hidden in her hands on the back of the toilet, smiled. Sex, sex, sex. There was nothing better than sex. Nothing better to help you forget your problems. He was just a boy, probably only in his early twenties. But boy or not, he still had all of the necessary equipment. He could still provide what she needed.

It had been so easy, seduction, it was always easy. She hadn't planned on being bent over a men's room toilet when she had walked into the bar. She had only come in for a drink after work. But then the gawky awkward looking kid had offered to buy her a drink and it only seemed fair to talk with him awhile. He was obviously a little drunk, but surprisingly funny and witty. He had told stories that reminded her of when she was younger, wilder, free. He had complimented her, told her she was pretty, admired her looks and her curves. She couldn't say at what point she had decided that she wanted to take him, but once decided, it was just a matter of time.

An accidental brush of the hand, an invasion of personal space, a caress of her hair, a licking of her lips. Her actions had spelled out only one conclusion. Finally when the bartender had gone into the backroom she could wait no longer. She had grabbed the pup by the hand and dragged him into the restroom. The nearest stall was all the privacy she needed. She was woman, hear her roar, she had to have her needs sated.

The boy continued to plunge himself into her rhythmically, her head softly bumping into the back wall, matching the beat. He wasn't a good lover, but he was enthusiastic. He wasn't as big as Grayden. Fuck. Why had she thought of that bastard? She tried to push the thought from her head. Fuck him, he didn't deserve her. He never complimented her, never made her feel beautiful. She spent a lot of time making herself beautiful. She knew she was no longer young. When she looked in the mirror she saw her sagging skin and eyes lined by crow's feet. She worked out all the time. She bought clothes to accentuate what she still had. She strategically placed makeup. She did everything she could.

But did Grayden notice? Fuck no. She had spent an entire hour that morning getting ready, making sure everything was just right. Did he notice? No, he just sat at the table, reading his newspaper. Once upon a time he would have taken one look at her and lost control. He would have ripped her blouse open and bent her over the kitchen table, his lusts undeniable. Not anymore. Now he did not see her that way. She had grown old. They were no longer young. To Grayden she might as well just be a vacuum cleaner, or a tube of toothpaste. His work and hobbies got his attention, not her.

The pup started moaning as he continued thrusting. Rita did not truly notice. She was aware that he was fucking her, she could feel him inside of her, but she took no pleasure from the experience. Her mind was firmly entrenched in its bitterness. She had been young once, and Grayden had loved her and wanted her so much. She had once been smooth skinned, with a tight ass and round pert tits. The boy had tried to take off her blouse, but she had stopped him. She did not want him to see how much her tits drooped, or how loose the skin around her belly had become. She didn't even know how the pup could stand to look at her cellulite riddled backside.

Fuck. It was ruined. The illusion was broken. She was still herself. She was not in her twenties anymore. She was just an old woman with an uncaring husband. She was used up, the best of her life already behind her. She could not escape it. The boy kept fucking. She wanted it to end. She tightened herself around him. The boy quivered and then spurt his seed with a groan. She pushed him out of her, quickly fixed her skirt, and turned around. For a moment she stared him in the eye. His puppy dog enthusiasm disgusted her. She disgusted herself. So many thoughts and feelings swirling in her head.

She had to get out. Rita pushed past the boy. Out of the stall. Out of the bathroom. Out of the bar. She hurriedly and stiffly walked to her car, unlocked the door, and got in. She put the key in the ignition, and broke down sobbing.

Chester

He slid it in. The woman groaned. Shuffling sounds, clothes against clothes, skin against skin, the sloppy clapping sounds that only mean one thing. Chester held his breath and hoped that nobody would notice him. The two in the next stall over had obviously been excited. So excited that they hadn't even stopped to check to see if anyone else was using the men's room.

Chester had never stopped at this bar before. In fact he rarely drank. When he was done with work he always went straight back home to Doris. But today had been different. Today had been different because he had decided to have a second helping of Doris' enchiladas last night at dinner. He should have known better, but Doris, for all of her shortcomings, was one hell of a cook. The enchiladas were delicious, but too many always carried a heavy price. He had tried to make it home. He had even run a few yellow lights, something he would never normally do, but in the end the needs of his body could not be ignored. He had to pull the car over at the first place he saw. Chester hated using public restrooms, but no thanks to those damn enchiladas he now found himself in a dingy dive bar bathroom, and now people were having sex in the next stall over.

The sound of thrusting from next door was punctuated by the raspy breathing of the woman and squishy sounds of her wetness. Chester grimaced. He hated sex. Chester's wife was fat, she had always been somewhat round, but middle age and good cooking had made her fat. Chester was frightened of his wife. Frightened of the day at least once a month when she came looking for him to fulfill his husbandly duties.

Chester did not dislike sex because his wife was fat. He had disliked sex when she was still just round. She had not been an unattractive round. In fact she had been such an attractive round that she had been very popular in college. In polite terms one would have called her a wild child. In more honest terms one would have probably called her a slut. Chester had wanted her, chased her, and inexplicably caught her. He had been part of the math club. She had slept with the football team. It went without saying that she had been, and still was, more experienced than him.

From the very first time Chester had lain with her he had felt like he could never fulfill her the way she had been fulfilled before. She had told him all about her past. Told him more than he wanted to know. That was probably part of the problem. Every time he tried to be sexual with her he couldn't get the image of all those men, the vast majority better looking and probably better endowed, doing all of those things to her. He was not a confident man. He was not a sexual man. He'd frankly just rather play backgammon.

The sounds from the next stall intensified. The woman was silent, but the man began to sound like a racehorse pulling toward the finish line. Sounds of separation. Rustling and adjustment. The sound of the woman leaving, a few minutes later the man following suit. Chester cleaned himself, flushed the toilet, left the bar, and went home. He prayed his wife would leave him alone tonight.

Roy

He slid it in. It fit perfectly. Roy smiled to himself as he fiddled with the knobs to pressurize the new keg he had just hooked up. It was Monday night, business was slow. Only two customers, and one guy who thought he had snuck in unseen to use the shitter without buying anything. Nothing new. It was unfortunate. Roy needed business to pick up. He had bills to cover, a loan to repay.

Roy shrugged to himself and walked back into the main room. The bar was empty. Where the twenty-something kid and middle-aged blonde had been sitting were just two empty mugs and some cash. Roy put the cash in the till and the mugs into the dishwasher and walked back into the backroom. If the bar was empty he might as well masturbate, at least it would help him forget about his problems. At least for a little while.

Our Mind

We think of ourselves as masters of our minds, but in truth it's our brains who are masters over us. Our brains take in the world around us and shape our perceptions of what we call reality. Our reality is a construct of the brain. Our minds are made up of the conscious, subconscious, and unconscious. The conscious is our thoughts, our memories, our wants, our problem solving computer. The subconscious is our primal urges, our dreams, our needs, our gut feelings. The unconscious is what runs our bodily functions, automatic, keeping us alive. The unconscious mind has no thought, it's only a constant background action. The conscious mind is logical, everything has rhyme and reason. The subconscious mind is illogical, it's reaction without reason, it's feeling without thought.

It's up to the conscious mind to make sense of what the subconscious mind is telling it. All of our perceptions first travel through our subconscious and then to our conscious. The subconscious adds a primal emotion, a gut reaction. The conscious mind then tries to make sense of all of the information it's given to find a logical course of action. The conscious mind uses our past memories to help it make its decisions. It compares the current situation to memories of situations from the past. It remembers and adjusts. It adapts to the world around it.

The subconscious also has a memory. The mind is a wonderful thing. It wants us to experience things that cause happiness, joy, and contentment. It wants us to avoid things that cause fear, anxiety, and anger. Like the conscious mind, the subconscious mind adapts to the world around it. When things make the world unpleasant for us it remembers. If certain things continually make the world unpleasant for us then it begins to ring the alarm bells. It begins to send us into a panic. The more we react to the panic the more it remembers to panic. The more it remembers to panic the stronger the panic becomes. We begin to avoid certain things, and the more we avoid them the greater the anxiety becomes. Over time the panic doesn't just drown out logic, it becomes logic.

Our subconscious is trainable. Just like Pavlov trained his dogs to salivate at the sound of a bell. We condition ourselves over time, and we don't even realize we're doing it. We do it until the gut feelings, which we've learned over our lives to trust, are wrong. Our subconscious is important, anxiety is meant to keep us safe and sound, but we can trick ourselves. We can teach our subconscious to protect us from things that aren't really dangerous. Salivating was a natural reaction to nearby food for the dogs. Their subconscious trained them to salivate at the sound of the bell, though they had no natural reason to do so without the food present. The subconscious is not logical. Its reactions don't always make sense.

The conscious mind is logical. It must take into account the outside input of perceptions and the primal reactions of the subconscious. If the reaction of the subconscious doesn't seem logical then the conscious mind struggles to make it logical. The brain is powerful, the brain is clever, the brain thinks that it is infallible, but it's not. When the conscious cannot make logical sense of the subconscious primal reaction, then the conscious must either challenge the subconscious and press forward, overcoming fear and anxiety again and again until the subconscious no longer negatively reacts to the stimuli, or it must alter how we perceive the world until it matches our subconscious reaction. This is how our reality is built by our mind.

An Unwanted Gift
Part 5

I don't meet the store clerk's eyes as he moves my purchases across the bar code reader. One bottle of rubbing alcohol. One bag of cotton balls. One bottle of hydrogen peroxide. One sleeve of small sewing needles. One bag of M&Ms. I keep my head down when I hand him the money, and don't look up until I'm safely back in my car. I drive home in silence, the radio switched off. I slowly eat the M&Ms as I drive, a treat for myself, a treat for what I have to do. The sky is clear. The sun is setting up ahead, ending a beautiful day in May. The last of the spring storms have blown on. It will be summer soon. At least I hope it will be.

Five treatments. Five treatments I have undergone over the past three months. Two different doctors have treated me and two different doctors have failed. I'm tired of failures. I'm tired of the burn of liquid nitrogen. Five treatments. Five failures. The molluscum reappear every time, just as numerous as the cold winter day in Kansas when I first discovered them. The bitter taste of disappointment permanently coats my mouth. The little red bumps laugh at me with their persistence. I'm no doctor, but even I have the sense to know that if something does not work five times, then a sixth will probably not do much better.

The molluscum controls my life now. Forcing every action to contend with its dominance. Each day when I shower I dry myself with a new towel. After my shower I put on a fresh pair of uncomfortable whitey tighties. I wear them to bed each night. I haven't worn underwear in three years. I haven't slept in clothes in even longer. I don't dare try to start a relationship with a woman. My life is devoid of intimacy. I don't even dare masturbate out of fear that it will spread the virus. The lack of release is starting to drive me mad. I think about it all the time, every second of every day. I keep getting uncontrollable hard-ons, often at the most awkward of times. I'm twelve again. Hormones rushing through me with wild abandon. I do my best to hide it. I do my best to live a perfectly normal life.

I have become an expert on molluscum contagiosum. A learned scholar of the subject. I have read articles from every conceivable source, from medical journals to homeopathic blogs. I've even gone as far as paying money to obtain a promised secret cure-all for my malady. A cure derived from household ingredients guaranteed to rid oneself of molluscum once and for all. I paid fifteen dollars for the suggestion of packing my groin with gauze soaked in apple cider vinegar for days on end. I haven't done it yet, but the idea has been given some serious consideration.

Molluscum contagiosum is caused by a virus that lives in the top layer of skin. The infected area develops a zit like bump which is called a molluscum. Just like a zit, when squeezed the molluscum ejects a hard white node and pus. It's in this node that the virus resides. Packing my junk with vinegar is not the only suggestion that I find on the internet. There is another more direct approach. One which I would have thought crazy a few months ago, but now seems to be possibly the only chance for salvation. I can't live my life like this anymore. I have to do something.

I walk into my house and turn the heater on in my bathroom. Summer may be starting, but it still gets chilly in the evenings. I pour some of the rubbing alcohol into a bowl and place three of the smaller sewing needles and a pair of tweezers in to disinfect them. The directions were very explicit on the need to maintain cleanliness. I take all of my supplies and place them in the bathroom. I strip down naked, except for a headlamp strapped to my forehead, and sit on my bath mat in a cross legged position, my back against the cold tub. I rub alcohol on my hands. The sharp odor tickles my nostrils. I'm ready to begin.

I turn on the headlamp. The shaft of light provides greater detail wherever it's pointed. My hands shake a bit as I grab one of the needles from the bowl. I slow my breathing and will my hand to hold still. My movements are slow. They must be sure. I blink my eyes a couple of times so they will better focus. They fall on the pearly head of a molloscum. A big ugly bastard midway up my shaft. One hand holds my member taut, the other maneuvers the needle just underneath the skin. It hurts, but not as much as I thought it would. You only have to break the skin at the top of the molloscum. The small wound begins to bleed. I put the needle back in the bowl of alcohol and grab the tweezers. I fish around in the wound. The tweezers re-emerge with a tiny hard white piece of matter stuck to their tip. I rub the tiny white piece of matter, teeming with virus, onto a square of toilet paper which I then throw into the toilet. Another square of toilet paper cleans the blood off of the tweezers before I put them back in the alcohol. I soak a cotton ball with hydrogen peroxide and press it against the wound until the bleeding stops.

The first one is done. Only thirty-two more to go. I don't think about what I'm doing. It all has an unreal quality to it. I'm neither patient or doctor. I do what has to be done. My shaft. My testicles. My legs. All is scoured in the pogrom which I've unleashed. All must be destroyed. All traces must be cleansed from the land.

It's not me in this place. I'm only an observer. A man without sin. Several times I pause to rewash my hands or scrub my entire groin area with alcohol, but I don't stop. It hurts. It hurts so very much. My eyes begin to water with tears. I wipe them clear, but I don't stop. The pain in my body is nothing compared to the uplifting of my soul. The feeling of returning hope. The rising anticipation that the nightmare might finally be over. I'm no longer a passive victim of my situation. I no longer have to depend upon heavenly volition brought about by prayer. No, I'm flying higher with every jab of the needle. My load is lightening with every exploration of the tweezers. I'm rising upward, and tomorrow it will be summer once again.

Some return, but much fewer than before. The moment they appear I cut them out just as I had the ones before. Twice more this happens over the next couple of weeks. It does not matter. I no longer carry with me the sense of defeat. The loss of hope. I know that I'm winning. I know that soon I will be clean.

Mandy

They stand looking at each other, the sun shining down giving false promise as the chill November wind blows through their jackets, clawing its way to their pink bodies beneath. Walking and idle chit chat has given way to silence. They look at each other, smiles upon their lips, but sadness in their eyes. They both knew when they started that it would have to come to an end. They both knew that this was not something that would last forever. Maybe that was why it had worked as well as it did? Maybe if things had been different they would have noticed each other's faults. It did not matter. That world did not exist. They could both pretend that it would have been perfect. It could be a happy haven for when their ships encountered stormy seas.

He reaches out and takes her hand lightly in his. There are so many things that he wants to say, so many things at the tip of his tongue. He had forgotten. Forgotten what it felt like to care about somebody for no other reason than they deserved to be cared for. Forgotten the feeling of contentment that comes from being with somebody you genuinely cherish. The feeling of knowing that they cherish you too. It had been a long time. He wants to thank her. Thank her for reigniting parts of him that he had long worried had fallen quiet and dead. Parts that he worried had been sacrificed in the pains of the past. The parts were still there. He could still be the man he once was. He could still be a better man than he had ever been.

He says nothing, just holds her hand in silence. He knows what he is. Just a temporary harbor. Just some silly man who had reached out and kissed somebody without really knowing why. Someone who did not judge and did not ask. A short respite from her own pains. She is a good person. One of the best he has met in a long time. Unlike many she does not put herself first. She understands the world beyond her own confines and cares how her actions affect it. She deserves to feel wanted, deserves to feel beautiful.

They lean together and awkwardly kiss. The action out in the wide world seems strange and out of place. Much more had been shared in their time together, no shame of being seen by others, no holding back when locked in their passion, but somehow, it is not the same at this moment. It has become a strange and foreign movement. They break apart and look at one another.

"My flight leaves in just a little bit," she says softly. "I guess this is goodbye."

"Have a good flight." Silence, words hanging unsaid.

She licks her lips and looks away for a second. "Well, goodbye then."

"Goodbye."

They separate and she walks away. He watches her get into her rented car and waves as she pulls out of the parking lot. He stands there for a bit, happy memories watered down by a feeling of loss. The best gift he has ever gotten, and he doesn't even know if she knows she has given it. He takes a deep breath, turns, and walks into his office building.

Empathy

It must have been hard for her. A traumatic event in her life, suddenly feeling overwhelmed, scared, no longer feeling the same lust that had once existed. Fear, wanting to pull away, but still caring very deeply for somebody, but at the same time, feeling nothing. It's a bad situation to be in, for rarely do we want to hurt other people, rarely do we stop caring about them once we've started, but our hearts are no longer in it. Sometimes we feel the need to pull away, to end things, because we perceive that if we continue, we will only cause a greater amount of pain.

Lord knows that I did not help. The hardest part is letting go, and I did not want to let go, so I fought it. I fought it harder than I had ever fought before. It must have been hard for her, being of two minds, one half wanting it to work, the other feeling like it never would and that every day prolonging it was just going to cause more hurt. Each day that I fought I became more emotionally invested. Each day that I fought it must have become harder for her, feeling like she should feel something, feeling nothing, fearing the pain she would have to cause. I should have let her go the first time she asked. Love is letting go to see if it comes back on its own. You can never force it.

It was hard for me. I had invested everything I had into it, went further than I had ever dared with any other. I let myself fall and did not try to stop myself, pushing past my fears and doubts. Love is in abundance in this world when one reaches out for it, when one lets go of themselves. I had touched paradise and I did not want to leave it. It hurt, to have my world come crashing down, to not understand what was happening. To work so hard and have her only return silence, to never say what was wrong. I was fighting a demon in the fog, slashing at shadows, not realizing that I just needed to drop my sword and walk away.

I feel for her. It is never easy to open up and talk about our emotions, especially ones that we know will hurt, will only be resisted. To speak of decisions we are not sure of ourselves. So we go silent, telling ourselves it does not matter. That speaking our minds will only cause us pain and do nothing to help the situation. This is not true. The truth will set us free. Silence may save us pain, but adds to the pain of the other. It will hurt, and likely fall on deaf ears, but we always owe the other the chance to understand, and likely when the dust has settled, they will remember, and find comfort.

It must have been hard for her. I forgive her.

Previously Published Works

My Guide To Initial Messages While Online Dating Part 1
First published at *www.thoughtcatlog.com*, Spring 2014

Doing What You Have To Do
First published in the *Soundings Review*, Summer 2015

The Care Package
First published in *Reading Hour*, Volume 5, Fall 2015

Home Sweet Home
First published in *China Grove*, Issue #4, Spring 2016

Attack
First published in the *Clackamas Literary Review*, Summer 2018

Dates Written

Angst	January 2011
Doing What You Have To Do	February 2013
The Golden Meadow	August 2010
On Top Of The World	August 2005
A Late Night Conversation	January 2011
The Care Package	September 2012
Junipers	January 2013
A Memory That Just Popped In My Head	October 2012
Heroes	November 2012
Major Wilkins Comes Home	September 2012
Memory	January 2013
An Awkward Black History Month	February 2013
Art	December 2012
My Guide To Initial Messages Part 1	October 2012
My Disinheritance	September 2012
Addiction	January 2013
How I was Almost Deaf	January 2013
Blow Job	February 2013
The Purpose Of Life	November 2012
The Colonel	August 2012
Golden Tears	September 2001
Characters	December 2012
Home Sweet Home	October 2012
Feverish Ramblings	January 2013
Totally Abnormal Childhood Memories	November 2012
Waiting	December 2012
An Unwanted Gift	March 2013
My Guide To Initial Messages Part 2	December 2012
Pineappaphilia	December 2012
Attack	February 2013
Mr. Campbell's Wild Ride	November 2012

Also Written By The Author

The Uncanny Valley

We all know a Paul. A person who seems to see stuff that isn't there. The type the polite call quirky and the blunt call nuts. Conspiracies? He's got a few. He's got his finger on how the world really works. He knows what kind of shit is coming down the pipe. Flee across the West Texas desert to Mexico? Makes sense to him. Feel like you're being watched? You bet your ass someone is watching. Best turn off your cellphone. Troubles? Of course, that's just part of life. Doubts? No time for doubts. Shit is getting real. Get in, buckle up, crack open a beer. The only real question is, how far down the rabbit hole are you willing to follow?

Available on Amazon, Barnes and Noble, Kobo, and Apple.

Professor Errare Presents...45 Jerks And Counting

The President of the United States of America. It has to be one of the hardest jobs in the world. You're under never ending pressure, you get blamed for everything, people hate your guts no matter what you do, and to top it all off, it ages you faster than meth. What kind of person would want a job like that? I'll tell you who, a jerk. The U.S. of A. has had 45 presidents so far in its history, and all have had one thing in common. They've all been jerks. This satirical book is not here to tell you about the great things that each president did. No, it's here to make you question how these people ever got to be leaders, and more importantly, what the hell is wrong with us for electing them. Enjoy.

Available on Amazon.

Professor Errare Presents…40 American Jackasses Worth Knowing

There is probably no greater American tradition than that of being a jackass. Where else in the world is a jackass truly free to reach their full potential of jackassery? Throughout our country's history men and women have risen to the braying call of infamy, willing to put it all on the line to prove…..well….. we're really not all that sure. This satirical book is here to tell you about some of the greatest of these All-American jackasses, with a few people who had to deal with everybody around them being a jackass thrown in for good measure. Read it, enjoy it, and perhaps even be inspired to find out just how much of a jackass you yourself can be.

Available on Amazon.

More information can be found at:

www.shawnwcampbell.com

About The Author

S.W. Campbell was born in Eastern Oregon in 1983 after a harrowing drive through a fog. He currently resides in Portland, Oregon where he works as an economist and lives with a lovely house plant named Morton. He has had several short stories published in various books, some of which appear in this work, and has also self-published several books. His work can be found at www.shawnwcampbell.com.

An Unsated Thirst